Christmas Home

A Windsor Peak Novel

Book 8

Denise Latham

Windsor Peak:

Coming Home

Staying Home

Finding Home

Forever Home

Holiday Home

You're Home

Our Home

Christmas Home

Windsor Peak: The Monahans

Healing Promise

Dedication

To all of you who love the holiday season, who know Hallmark movies by heart, and who embrace the magic.

And to my parents, who taught me that a Christmas tree falling over was just a normal part of the holiday!

Chapter 1

"Happy Thanksgiving, my love." Patrick Burrows kissed his sleeping girlfriend on the forehead. "I'm headed out to the Turkey Trot, I'll meet you after."

"Wait," Emma said sleepily, pulling him close for a hug. "I was going to come with you."

"I know, but you were up late getting ready for today," he said. "Sleep, and I'll see you at the Palace later."

He slipped out of the bedroom and closed the door behind him, happy to see that she had put her head back down. Emma had been burning the candle at both ends for weeks, helping with the rescue animals that had recently arrived while also preparing for Thanksgiving. He knew that she had spent the better part of the last week going through Christmas decorations in the garage, although she had resisted the urge to start decorating. He knew if they weren't hosting today, they would be halfway to Christmas by now, at least in terms of decor.

Driving down the mountain from his house, he saw the crowds already gathered in the street. As a movie star, he was used to public attention, but he usually avoided it in his small hometown of Windsor Peak. Days like today were the exception, when he would allow himself to be a spectacle to help raise money for the town. The Turkey Trot was the annual race held on Thanksgiving morning, which raised money for town funds that supported the local school, youth center and library. He had let it slip intentionally in an interview that he would be running this race along with his co-star in a massively popular superhero movie franchise. The race registrations had immediately tripled, and Patrick knew even more people would cram the streets of the town to catch a glimpse of them. It was good for town businesses, and the small Inn had sold out completely within minutes of the news being released.

As he parked in the small lot behind the restaurant his sister-in-law owned, he spotted his brothers climbing out of a truck across the lot. Dan, the oldest, had ridden down with their middle brother, Jake. Patrick watched as Jake opened the back door of the truck and let his service dog, Rex, out of the truck. Rex had done wonders to help Jake deal with the PTSD that he struggled with after years in the military. An event like the run, with crowds of people, would have been difficult for him in the past, but Rex made it possible now.

"Morning," Patrick called over to them as he got out of his car. "Cold start today."

"It's not too bad," Dan said. "Anything above ten degrees is fine with me."

"Where's Liam? I thought you would ride together," Jake asked as they approached. Patrick's fellow movie star, and co-star in the movie franchise, had recently moved to Windsor Peak full time and was running with him in the charity race. It was typically easier for them to arrive at big events together, so that any chaos could be controlled easily.

"Mike was picking him up," Patrick answered. Their friend and personal trainer, Mike, was going to run with them, which would help with the crowd control and motivate them to keep their pace. Mike was a former professional football player and still gave off the sense that he would happily tackle anyone who got in his way.

"Does that mean I'm not on personal protection duty?" Jake asked, glancing over at Patrick as they walked toward the back door of the restaurant.

"You have better observation skills than Mike, thanks to the years in the military," Patrick replied. "I'd still like it if you stayed close, but if you'd rather not, I get it."

"No, it's fine," Jake said. "You just slow me down."

"Unlikely," Patrick said. "I'm in much better shape."

"You're both going to lose to me anyway," Dan said, pulling the door open and waving for them to go through first.

"Doubtful," Patrick said.

"You've been getting slower in your old age," Jake commented.

"You're two years younger than me," Dan said back. "Watch yourself."

"Morning, boys," Zoe, Emma's sister and the head chef at the restaurant, greeted them as they entered through the kitchen door. She was married to the town sheriff, JJ, who was one of Patrick's closest friends. "Everyone is out front."

"Thanks, Zoe," Patrick said. He stayed behind as his brothers passed through the door so he could speak to Emma's sister for a moment. "You'll be by later with JJ?"

Zoe nodded. "We're going to have his family over for dinner, but I talked to Emma about us stopping by your house before they come. We'll be up to see you guys right after JJ's done with the football game and the race."

"Perfect," Patrick said. "I feel like I haven't seen him in a while."

"Between the Harvest Festival and the events today, he's pretty busy," Zoe said.

"Alright, it will be good to catch up. Emma will be in soon. I think she was going to sleep a little longer," Patrick said.

"Go grab some food before you head out," Zoe said, pointing at the main dining room. "If your brothers leave you anything."

"It was nice of you to open early and feed us," Patrick called over his shoulder as he headed out.

"You can thank Kendra for that," Zoe said with a laugh.

Sure enough, Dan's wife Kendra was in the dining room, handing out drinks from behind the bar. Dan and Jake each had plates filled with the buffet offerings. Patrick quickly filled a plate with fresh fruit and grabbed a yogurt before joining them.

"No carbs?" Dan asked, glancing between his pastry-loaded plate and Patrick's.

"I start filming in a little less than two months," Patrick said. "I need to be ready."

"Those tights show everything," Jake said to Dan.

"Spandex," Patrick replied automatically, used to his brother's teasing.

"Is Emma going with you next week?" Dan asked.

"I didn't know you were going anywhere," Jake said. "All you've been talking about is how excited you are to have a great holiday season here in town before you have to leave to film another movie."

"I have to fly out to California on Friday," Patrick said. "Just do some voiceover stuff for the last movie, and fittings for the upcoming shoot. And a lot of press."

"Friday? I thought you were going on Monday?" Dan asked.

"Me too," Patrick said. "Next thing I knew, the studio was sending a plane for me, Liam and Natalie tomorrow. It certainly made their lives easier when Natalie moved here as well, so they can put us all on the same flight."

"That's weird," Dan said. "They don't usually want you to work over the weekend."

"I know," Patrick said. He thought back to what he had discussed with his manager and heard from his friends who were also involved. Natalie was the main female star of the movie series and always got handed a brutal schedule. The three main men could split up the press duties, but Nat had no one to share with when they wanted a female. She was also always in high demand for advertising spots, which would be divided up among the three men if they wanted a male. "Nat has a bunch of press scheduled and, apparently, a gigantic wardrobe that needs to be altered for her. Luckily for all of us, she was pretty demanding about how long she would stay out there, and she wants to spend as much time in Windsor Peak for Christmas as possible. I think we're all just working around her schedule while we're out there."

"As always." Liam's voice came from behind him, and Patrick turned to see his co-star along with Mike.

"Watch yourself," Mike practically growled at Liam. Natalie had moved to Windsor Peak almost a year before, after falling in love with the hulking trainer. He was fiercely protective of her and didn't ever want Nat to be upset.

"She knows," Liam argued. "It's not my fault that she's more popular than us. I do half the photo shoots she does."

"Well, you're much uglier," Mike muttered under his breath as he took a seat at the table.

"You're lucky I have a healthy dose of self-confidence," Liam said. "Someone else might take offense and need to do something about that."

"Healthy? More like overabundance," Mike replied. "And I'd like to see you try."

"Please, try," Jake said. "I want to record it so I can cheer myself up anytime I need to."

"Boys, enough fighting," Kendra called out. "You have ten minutes until they want you at the starting line. JJ asked that you go first, so it's easier to keep an eye on the two of you."

Patrick nodded and finished his fruit, carrying his empty plate to deposit on the bar. Jake followed, leaning against the bar and studying his brother. "You seem off today," he said. "What's up?"

"Me? Nothing," Patrick replied. At his brother's knowing look, he sighed. "Maybe it's just knowing that I'm leaving tomorrow."

"You don't usually mind," Jake said.

"I know," Patrick said. "But it's Emma's favorite time of the year, and I'm going to be across the country."

"It's not like you're missing Christmas," Jake said. "It's still a few weeks away. You'll be back in plenty of time."

"You're right," Patrick said. "It's that, plus the stories that have been running. I didn't want to bring her to Los Angeles and have her deal with the press, but I worry about leaving her alone. I don't care what they say about me, but it bothers me that they attack her."

"We'll keep a close eye on her," Dan promised. "If anyone shows up here, we can always have her come stay with us."

"She'll want to be at the house with the horses," Patrick said. "But if you can keep an eye out, that would help. I know it's bothering her, and she doesn't want to say anything."

"What are they saying? I don't read the gossip rags," Jake said.

"It's everything from saying we broke up, to me cheating, and back to the speculation that she's a gold digger," Patrick said. "It's exhausting."

"When you get back, we can plan a night to come to Christmas Karaoke," Jake said. "That will cheer Emma right up and take your minds off the nasty reporters."

"Good idea. And I'll need to borrow your truck to pick up a tree, the first chance we get after I fly back," Patrick said. "Making her wait is adding to my stress, so I'll want to do that as soon as we fly home."

"I can get it for you, have it set up to decorate when you get home," Jake offered.

"No, Emma wants us to pick it out together," he said. "But I appreciate the offer."

"You two ready to go?" Dan asked, placing his dirty plate on the bar.

Patrick glanced around, not seeing Emma anywhere. "I was hoping Emma would be here by now," he told his brothers. "She must have fallen back into a deep sleep and forgotten to set an alarm."

The three brothers walked outside, along with their friends, to find a large crowd. Patrick watched as the murmur ran through the crowd as he and Liam stepped into sight, and a plethora of cameras were turned to face the duo. The people closest to the restaurant all clamored to get closer, but were deterred by JJ and his fellow officers, who helped them make their way to the starting line.

"Patrick!" The sound of his voice being called came from every direction, but his ear caught the sound of Emma's voice from somewhere in the crowd. Glancing around, he saw her waving from the back, blocked in by walls of people.

"Mike," Patrick said, stopping to turn around to face his trainer. "Emma is back there."

Mike looked where Patrick pointed and nodded. Within a minute, he had made his way through the crowd to where she stood and then came back with her just as quickly. Emma quickly made her way to Patrick, wrapping her arms around his waist and hugging tight.

"I wanted to wish you luck," she said. "But the traffic was so bad, I had to park a few blocks away and couldn't make it to the restaurant."

He leaned down to kiss her, already feeling calmer in her presence. "I was just starting to worry," he said. "I'm glad you made it. Do you want Mike to help you get over with everyone else?"

"I'll be okay," she said. "People are trying to get close to you, not me. I'll see you at the Palace after."

With another quick kiss, she let him go, and he watched as she weaved her way through the runners to get to the front porch of the Palace. Once there, she waved to him and blew a kiss, so he could turn his attention back to the run ahead.

"If you're all ready, I'll get you started now." The mayor, Charlotte Bryant, was standing directly in front of Patrick once he turned back around. She was no more than five feet tall and had been in charge of the town for as long as he could remember. No one knew how old she was, or dared to cross her, as far as he knew. She was tiny but powerful and fought hard for the town of Windsor Peak when necessary.

"We're ready," he told her.

With a nod, she walked away and climbed the steps to the small stage set just beside the starting line. She tapped on the microphone, looking satisfied when the crowd quieted quickly. "Happy Thanksgiving," she said. "And thank you all for participating in our annual Turkey Trot. This race helps to raise a lot of money for the town, and this year in particular, we are grateful to have two of our resident celebrities here to kick off the race. Patrick and Liam, if you're ready, we'll get you to do the ceremonial start to the race."

Their small group stepped forward, and the mayor counted them down before blowing an air horn that sounded like a turkey gobble. As soon as he started running, Patrick was able to lose his thoughts about what was coming the next day. Focusing on the sound of his feet on the pavement, the company of the men around him, and the cheers from fans on the street helped reset his mood.

Chapter 2

Emma chewed on her nail anxiously as she looked at the food that was on the kitchen counter, courtesy of her sister, Zoe. "I don't think I can do this," she said. "You can't leave me."

"I have to," Zoe said. "We're hosting JJ's family. Remember, I invited you all to come there?"

"That would have been too many people," Emma said. "The Burrows are a lot, and when you combine with JJ's whole family plus Liam and Holly, it's way too much."

"We could have fit," Zoe said, then laughed. "Actually, no. We all would have needed to come here, because it's so much bigger. But this is fine. Everything is cooked and ready to just be heated up. I labeled it all for you. It's foolproof."

"You say that as if I'm not a fool," Emma said.

Zoe laughed again, turning as the sound of JJ and Patrick came from the stairs. Patrick had taken JJ down to show him a new piece of gym equipment that had been delivered, which all the men seemed very excited about. Emma did her best to avoid the gym, preferring yoga or walks outside to the weights and machines Patrick needed to keep in shape for his movies.

"Thanks for doing all this, Zoe," Patrick said, indicating the turkey and fixings on the island. "I hope you don't mind if I tell my brothers I did it all."

"Go for it," Zoe replied. "Somehow I think they'll figure it out pretty quickly."

"We did the desserts," Emma said, snuggling close to Patrick. "That counts for something."

"What time are you having family over?" Patrick asked JJ and Zoe. "Do you have time for a drink?"

"No," JJ said. "I still need to swing back through town quickly to make sure everything is quiet, and then can head to the house. The family is coming at two, so we're cutting it close. But we wanted to talk to you both privately."

"Oh, is everything okay?" Emma asked, immediately worried about her sister.

"Everything is fine," Zoe assured her. She exchanged a smile with JJ before looking back at Emma and Patrick. "More than fine, actually. We're having a baby."

"What? I'm going to be an aunt?" Emma rushed over to hug Zoe, tears falling freely as she did. "Oh, Zoe, I'm so happy for you! How do you feel?"

"Tired," Zoe said with a laugh. "But the first trimester is almost over, and the doctor said that it should improve."

Patrick was hugging JJ, then switched places with Emma so she could do the same. JJ wiped back a tear of his own and grinned at Emma. "I'm taking good care of her, I promise. Regular foot rubs," he said. "And I've gotten her to switch from coffee to herbal tea."

"That part is terrible," Zoe said. "But it's okay. Whatever will keep the baby healthy is fine."

"You're sure everything is good?" Emma asked, looking at her sister with worry. Zoe had suffered a miscarriage six months prior, and it had been hard of her emotionally. Emma had spent several nights at their house, not wanting to be far away from her sister if she needed her.

"The doctor said everything is fine," Zoe assured her. "I just saw them again last week, and the ultrasound showed everything is perfect."

"Do you know if it's a boy or a girl?" Patrick asked.

"No," JJ responded. "We decided to wait and find out."

"I love it no matter what," Emma said. "Does your family know yet?"

"We'll tell them today," JJ said. "Zoe had some T-shirts made up for them, labeling them as grandparents, aunt, uncles. But we didn't know what to call old Patrick here, so we didn't get you one."

"I'm an uncle too, aren't I?" Patrick asked, a confused look on his face.

"Put a ring on it, man," JJ said, punching his friend lightly in the arm. "You don't get to avoid that just because you're super famous."

"Don't pressure him," Emma said quickly.

"No pressure, just teasing," JJ said. "I'm sure you'll be official by the time the baby is born."

"Nothing like putting a clock on it," Patrick replied. Emma studied his face, unable to read the expression. He could mask his thoughts well, given his years of practice in acting. Was he bothered by JJ's comment?

"Back to the baby," Emma said, needing to steer the conversation back on track. "JJ's family is going to freak out."

"They will," JJ said. "My parents have been hinting about a grandchild for a while now. I can only imagine how crazy they will be over the next six months."

"It's so nice you'll have all of them here," Emma said to Zoe. "Especially since it's just the two of us in our little family. Well, I guess your mom too, Zoe."

"She was barely a mom, never mind a grandma," Zoe said with an eye roll. "But who knows. She has been reaching out more often."

"Maybe she'll surprise us," JJ said, reaching over to squeeze his wife's hand. Zoe's relationship with her mother was complicated to say the least, and JJ had been supportive in whatever happened. Zoe was still upset at her mother's role in Emma being thrust into foster care when her own mother had died. In Zoe's opinion, Emma should have come to live with her half-sister, and no amount of explanation from her mother could justify the decisions that were made. Emma had tried to tell Zoe that she forgave the other woman, but it wasn't enough for her sister.

"Well, the baby has amazing grandparents with JJ's mom and dad," Zoe said. "And more than enough aunts and uncles. Not to mention, the whole town of Windsor Peak feels like family at this point."

"Did you tell Kendra yet?" Emma asked, referring to Kendra's business partner.

"Not yet, but I think she suspects. I've been struggling in the kitchen with some foods," Zoe said. "And taking more breaks than usual."

"Still working more than you probably should be," JJ said.

"The doctor said it's fine," Zoe replied. "It's good for me to be active."

"Speaking of, we should get going," JJ said. "Our day is jam-packed, and we're cutting it close. I don't want my brothers arriving before us, they'll eat half the food and claim they didn't know better."

"Alright," Zoe said. She hugged Emma tightly. "Want me to come over tomorrow, and we can do some online shopping?"

"Yes," Emma said. "Patrick leaves early in the morning, so I'll be bored and alone. And I need some help thinking of gift ideas for the man who has everything."

"The man who has everything because he has you," Patrick said, pulling Emma close to kiss her on the head. "I don't need anything else."

"Should I mention the ring again?" JJ whispered to Zoe loudly enough for everyone to hear, making her laugh.

"I heard you the first time," Patrick said, his tone tight.

They said goodbye and watched as Zoe and JJ disappeared through the front door. The minute it closed behind them, the silence seemed heavy, and Emma suddenly felt uncomfortable. Would Patrick think she had put the idea of a ring in JJ's head? Would he think she had been complaining to her sister about it?

Before she could address it, Patrick pulled her towards the kitchen and the trays of food sitting out. "We should put this food away. Tell me what can go into the refrigerator in the garage and I'll start moving it."

They moved quickly through the items, putting the turkey in the oven to warm up according to Zoe's instructions, and the rest of the food away. Once it was clear, she looked around, seeing they were more than ready for his family to arrive. The table was set, bottles of wine and soda were on the counter, and the house was spotless. They had both showered and changed after the Turkey Trot, so all they had to do was wait.

"Want me to put the parade on TV?" Patrick asked, gesturing to the large screen above the fireplace.

"If you want," Emma said. "But, first..."

"What?"

"Should we talk about what JJ just said? I feel like it might be awkward if we don't," Emma said.

"About the ring?"

"Yes."

Patrick scratched his head and avoided her eyes. "We can if you want to," he said. "I just feel like—"

The doorbell rang, interrupting whatever he had been about to say. They stood staring at each other for a moment before he motioned at the door. "I should let them in."

Emma nodded. "Yes," she said.

"We can talk about it later," he said, just before opening the door. "I promise."

He pulled the door open, revealing his parents, Ben and Stella. They hugged Patrick as they came in, then Stella embraced Emma as the two men talked. "We wanted to come a little early, just in case you needed help," she said. "But it looks like you have everything under control. It looks and smells amazing in here."

"Thanks," Emma said. "I can only take credit for the table. Zoe did all the cooking and dropped it off a few minutes ago."

"One less thing for you to worry about," Stella said, patting her on the arm. "We brought some pies. Ben will have the boys get them out of the car for us."

"You didn't have to do that," Emma said. "You should be resting. It's only been a few weeks since you finished your chemotherapy treatments."

"All the more reason to keep busy," Stella said. "You face cancer and win, and everything in life feels a little sweeter. Especially apple pie."

The doorbell rang again, and Patrick let in his two brothers and their families. Jake, along with his wife Shea, teenage son Charlie and baby daughter Isobel, arrived in a blur of noise. As soon as they were settled, Dan, Kendra, eight-year-old Calle and baby Declan made their arrival. The room was filled with happy voices and the kind of chaos a big family creates, and Emma felt a hint of something sad in her heart. She loved these people, and they had come to be family for her, but they weren't officially hers. Not yet, anyway. If something went wrong between her and Patrick, she wouldn't just lose him. She'd lose all of them.

Battling back tears that had sprung out of nowhere, she hurried to the kitchen to pretend the turkey needed to be checked on. No one seemed to notice as they all greeted each other, so she had a moment to grab a tissue and wipe at her eyes.

"Are you crying?" Calle's voice came from behind her, the sound loud enough to carry two towns over. It seemed like the whole room stopped talking at once and turned to look at Emma.

"Tears of joy," she said, forcing a smile on her face. "I'm so happy to be here with you all."

Calle wrapped her legs around Emma's waist and squeezed. "I almost had those tears today," she said. "I saw Santa on the TV and got really excited. But Mama said I might wake up Declan, and I needed to quiet down."

"Santa was in the parade," Kendra explained, hugging Emma quickly. "We had it on as we all got ready, and the scream she let out could have woken the dead. Fortunately, Declan sleeps through anything. Actually, she probably gets credit for that. He's so used to the noise his sister makes, he sleeps through anything."

"Lucky," Emma said. "I feel like I wake up ten times a night."

Kendra frowned as she looked at her. "Are you okay?"

"I am," Emma said, nodding. "I promise."

"I know the stories are getting to you. I almost lost it last week when I saw the article claiming Patrick was having an affair with Nat. It's so lazy of them to keep running with the story. Jut because they are good friends and co-stars doesn't mean they are romantic. Why can't they just leave you all alone? If you ever need to talk, you know how to reach me," Kendra said.

"Me too," Shea chimed in from behind them. Emma turned and accepted a hug from Jake's wife.

"Thanks," she said. "Patrick is leaving tomorrow, and I'm feeling more unsettled than usual. These stories don't help. His team keeps telling me it's normal, with a new movie coming out, but I'm not used to being in the spotlight. All these people talking about me online as if they know me is a lot to take in. I'm just a little overwhelmed by it all."

"It could also be the holidays that's upsetting you," Shea said. "Especially after everything you went through as a kid. It would be totally normal to get emotional this time of year."

"I do miss my mom," Emma admitted. "I wish she could have met him, and all of you."

"I'm glad you have Zoe," Kendra said. "I know you two are tight, but Shea and I want to be there for you as well. And if you need us to take on any nasty reporters, just say the word."

"I'm down to fight. I'm small, but scrappy. And if you don't mind total chaos, you're welcome to stay with Jake and I while Patrick is away," Shea offered. "It's hockey season, so Charlie leaves wet gear everywhere to dry. The smell is horrific, but if I touch it, I could cause his team to lose, apparently. And Isobel is teething. But we could have fun."

"Thanks," Emma said with a smile. "I'll stay here. We have some new rescues in the barn, and I like to keep an eye on them. And he's only going to be gone for a week at the most."

Emma listened as the two women started chatting about the stages the two youngest were in, her eyes drifting over to where Patrick was huddled with his two brothers near the fireplace. She couldn't hear what they were talking about, but Patrick looked serious and Dan was frowning. Could he be sharing what JJ had said? The thought of him feeling pressure to propose made her feel a little sick, but the thought that he didn't want to marry her at all made her feel even worse.

Chapter 3

"Nat thinks they're going to try to keep us in Los Angeles for longer than a week," Patrick told his brothers. "I know my contract specifies that I have to do all the voice work and interviews on their schedule, but is there any way to push back on it?"

Dan frowned, considering the question. In addition to being his oldest brother, Dan was his lawyer and knew the paperwork backwards and forward. "I'll reach out to them tomorrow," he said. "You never ask for much, so I can't see it being a problem. Why not have Emma just go with you, though?"

"She wants to be here, with Zoe," Patrick said, keeping the secret they had been told earlier to himself. JJ was a friend to all of them, and he didn't want to spill before it was made public. "Plus, I want to keep her out of the spotlight. The press has been brutal to her lately, and if they can just focus on me, that will alleviate some pressure. Not to mention, she loves Christmas and doesn't want to be in sunny California when it should be cold and snowy. Not being able to decorate tomorrow is already killing her, never mind if I get stuck out there even longer."

"I'll work it out with the producers," Dan promised. "I'll make sure that they get you done on time."

"You sure you don't want me to get you a tree tomorrow?" Jake offered. "Then you can decorate it as soon as you get back."

"No, she wants us to pick it out together," Patrick said. "And I agree. We could have a team of decorators fly in and take care of everything, but half the fun is doing it ourselves. I want this holiday to be really special for her."

"Any particular reason?" Jake asked, with an eyebrow raised.

"No," Patrick said quickly. "She does so much for me, and for everyone else. This is her favorite time of the year, and I want to share it with her. Not to be stuck in California smiling for cameras, being poked with pins and doing the same interviews."

"Got it," Jake said. He looked over at where his son Charlie was entertaining the two babies and his cousin Calle. "I'm going to give Charlie a hand. He looks a little overwhelmed. One teenager to two babies is a bad enough ratio, never mind when you mix in the second grader who thinks he should focus only on her."

Patrick watched as Jake settled onto the couch, his service dog sitting by his feet. Isobel tottered over with a book in hand, gesturing to be picked up. Declan tried to climb up as well, not wanting to be far from his cousin, and Dan swept in to settle him on his lap. The two babies were engrossed in the book Jake held, while Calle applied play makeup to Charlie's face. The two babies were engrossed in the book Jake held, while Calle applied play makeup to Charlie's face. Emma was deep in conversation with his two sisters-in-law and Stella in the kitchen, his father walking away from them to join Patrick.

"You look deep in thought," Ben said. "What's on your mind?"

"I hate that I have to leave tomorrow," he admitted. "And I was just thinking about all of this."

"All of what?"

"This," Patrick said, gesturing to the room. "Being settled down. Family, children. A quiet life."

"You have a lot of that now," Ben said. "You've spent more time here over the last two years than since you were a kid. You and Emma seem solid. Are you saying you're ready to make things permanent and think about kids?"

"I think so," Patrick said. "Is that crazy? Is it fair to do it to Emma?"

"Do what to Emma?"

"Put all that pressure on her," he said. "It's been so hard lately, and it would be so much worse. Think about what it would be like if we were engaged and then getting married. She'd be followed constantly and criticized like crazy. She hates the attention and can't read the comments on anything because people are so nasty. Having to do that forever might be hard for her."

"A few things," Ben said slowly. "First, you can't predict what the future will bring. Worrying about that makes as much sense as watching the weather, when you just know it's going to be wrong. Look what happened to me. One minute I was happily married to your mother and having my third child, and the next I was a widow. I never would have thought I would end up raising you three with Stella, but that's what life had in store for me."

"That's different," Patrick said. "You didn't worry about my mom dying. If you had known she would die when having me, would you have prevented it from happening?"

"No," Ben said. "There would have been no changing her mind about having another baby, and I would never for one second regret having you. And the happiness that I have with Stella is different, although I can't explain how. But I can't look back and question what my relationship was like with your mom compared to your stepmother. That's unfair to both of them. Long story short, you can't control what life hands you, so stop worrying about it."

"It's different when it's other people talking about us," Patrick said. "We know how we feel, but the entire world feels like they are entitled to an opinion on our relationship."

"Well, that's my second point. No one who loves you both believes one word of what they publish. You can't let other people's opinions dictate how you live your life. And finally, most importantly, she loves you. If she were going to be scared off by all of this, she would have already left. She's tougher than she looks, don't discredit her."

"I'm not, I just know that a life with me means constant scrutiny, and I know she's been struggling with it lately," he said. "Not knowing who your friends are, or who just wants something from you. It means she could one day be alone with a baby while I'm busy in another country."

"All things she knows about already," Ben said. "And she won't be alone. Look around the room at all the people she has, plus Zoe. Anyway, I think you're looking at it from the wrong angle."

"How so?"

"You're looking at the negatives, and that's not like you. You're usually a glass half full kind of guy," Ben said. "Think about what you both gain from this. Commitment, love, family, and knowing that you're going through it all together. That's all worth it, in my opinion."

"I suppose you're right."

"You know I am," Ben said. "I always am. And I'd like to point out one more thing."

"What's that?"

"You could walk away from Hollywood anytime you want," Ben said. "You have enough money already. There's no reason you can't just enjoy a quiet life here."

"I'd be disappointing a lot of people if I did that," Patrick points out.

"But that's not your responsibility," Ben said.

"I know," Patrick said. "But I do love it. I've really dialed it back this year, and I like the speed better. I'd like to do another Broadway run maybe, and Jake and I have been talking about recording an album together. I'm looking forward to all of that, but I know I'm not ready to walk away from movies just yet."

"As long as you're doing it because you love it," Ben said.

"I am," Patrick said with a nod. "Taking me out to California all those years ago was the greatest thing you've ever done for me. I don't know if I've ever said it before, but thank you. I complain a lot, but I'm living a pretty amazing life because of you taking that chance on me."

"And now you can pay it forward," Ben said, gesturing toward Emma with his chin. "Think of all she's been through. You can give her what she's been missing for so long. Family, stability. Love."

Emma glanced over, as if sensing the men talking about her, and smiled. It looked uncertain, as if the turmoil he was feeling about leaving her the next day was upsetting her as well. He kicked himself mentally for allowing his feelings to ruin one of her favorite days, and the last they would spend together for a week. Today kicked off the Christmas season, and she had been looking forward to it. And here he was, pouting and putting a damper on it. Time to shift his attitude and focus on making everything perfect for her.

The doorbell rang again, indicating the last guests to join them had arrived. Patrick's co-stars, Natalie and Liam, were joining them with their significant others. The trip to California had spoiled Natalie and Mike's plans to spend Thanksgiving in New Hampshire with his family, so they had readily accepted an invitation. Liam was dating Shea's sister, Holly, so they were essentially family as well. The foursome came into the room wearing Santa hats and in good moods, and Patrick was determined to match their spirits.

***

"Should we go around the table and say what we're thankful for?" Charlie asked as they all sat down at the long table for dinner. Patrick was seated at the end of the table, with Emma at his side. It had taken everyone, minus the three youngest, to get all the food on the table. Zoe had made enough to feed an entire movie set, and then some.

"I think we're all grateful for this feast," Jake said.

"And for this amazing family," Shea added.

"Good health," Ben said, reaching over to squeeze Stella's hand.

"Football," Mike added. At Natalie's elbow jab to his ribs, he laughed. "And love."

"A long weekend away from school," Charlie said, making Calle cheer. "What are you thankful for, Calle?"

"Santa Claus," Calle said. "He's coming soon."

"He is," Emma said, glowing at the little girl. "I can't wait."

"And Auntie Shea is having another baby," Calle said. "I want another one too, so I think I'll ask Santa for a baby."

Dan cleared his throat at the end of the table, pulling everyone's attention to him and Kendra. They were smiling at each other, causing the rest of the table to start laughing. "Are you?" Shea cried out, grabbing her sister-in-law's arm.

"I am," Kendra said. "But I guess we should have saved the news for Christmas. That would have saved us some shopping if that's all Calle wants."

"Really, mama? Another baby?" Calle jumped out of her seat, almost knocking over her plate of food in her hurry to get to her mother.

"Yes, honey," Kendra said.

"We couldn't let Jake outdo us," Dan added.

"Is it a girl?" Calle asked, looking hopeful.

"We don't know," Kendra replied.

"Can we please find out this time?" Calle begged her parents. "No offense to Declan, but I want a sister."

"We'll see if we can put in a special order," Dan said. "No, go eat, or Charlie will finish your plate too."

The teenager grinned down at his uncle, a bite of turkey halfway to his mouth. "I learned early with this family to eat while it's hot. And go for seconds before anyone else."

"Smart boy," Ben said, grinning at his grandson. "I'd like to make a toast, before we all dig in like Charlie. To our family and all those we love, to good friends, to our health, and that we may all remain as full of joy as we are right now in all the days going forward."

"Here, here," Patrick called back, raising his glass to clink with those around him. Everyone followed suit, smiling and laughing as they did. As his eyes met Emma's, he saw her love, mixed with something he couldn't quite put his finger on. He leaned closer so that he could speak to her. "Are you okay?"

"Yes," she whispered back. "Just grateful that you share all of this with me."

"You're a part of it too," he said. "They all might love you more than they do me."

"Knock it off," she said with a light laugh. "You know that's not true. But I do love them all."

She turned to clink glasses with Shea, who was next to her, and the moment was lost. He made a mental note to follow up with her later and finish their earlier conversation while he was at it. The last thing he wanted was for her to feel uncertain, especially at Christmas.

Chapter 4

Zoe arrived at the door early on Black Friday, carrying two to-go cups from the local coffee shop and a pastry bag from their friend Piper's bakery. Emma had worked there when she first came to town and was transported back to those days by the sweet smell coming from the bag. Something nutty and maybe with a hint of cinnamon, if her nose wasn't failing her.

"You're up early," Emma said as she took the hot cups from her sister.

"I have to pee every twenty seconds," Zoe replied. "This baby seems to use my bladder as a trampoline. And please don't remind me that it's only going to get worse as I get bigger, because that's what everyone says."

"I won't," Emma promised. "I have no experience to go off, so I have no idea, anyway. You aren't even showing, so I'm surprised the baby is already causing you issues."

"Happy ones, I swear," Zoe said. "After having the miscarriage, any sign that I'm pregnant is a good one. Even the throwing up."

"Were you very sick?"

"Constantly," Zoe said. "I have no idea why they call it morning sickness. I wish it were only in the morning."

"But it's better now?" Emma asked, worried about her sister. Zoe was always too driven to rest properly, and although she ate healthily, she tended to forget if she was busy in the kitchen. And drinking water was an afterthought, especially when lost in the process of cooking.

"It is. And I know what you're worrying about, so stop. I'm fine," Zoe said. "I had one little fainting spell a few weeks ago when I was dehydrated, so I've been lectured enough to listen. I even have a big jug of water I carry everywhere now."

Emma watched as Zoe pulled out a giant water bottle from her bag and then laughed. "No wonder you're needing to use the bathroom every ten seconds. That's enough water for an elephant."

"Don't start with those jokes," Zoe warned her.

"Never," Emma said. "You're glowing, and I know you're going to be radiant throughout the entire pregnancy. Is JJ overjoyed?"

"I think that's an understatement. He's beside himself. I wake up some nights and he's just staring at me, smiling," Zoe said. "He talks to my belly all the time, says he wants the baby to recognize him instantly. And he was amazing when I was so sick, he took such good care of me. I'm a lucky woman."

"And to think, you almost let him get away," Emma teased her sister.

"Fortunately, he's persistent, and was going to get his way," Zoe said. She pulled a plate out of the cabinet and started unloading pastries from the bag. "Piper had croissants right out of the oven. I know you love the almond ones, so I got some of those, plus chocolate. And she had these amazing cinnamon buns with pecans. I couldn't resist."

"That looks amazing," Emma said. "We can't possibly eat all of this."

"I'm pregnant," Zoe said. "It's entirely possible."

"I still can't believe I'm going to be an aunt," Emma said. "I feel like one to Patrick's nieces and nephews, but this will be different. Official."

"I hope JJ didn't make things awkward for you yesterday. I couldn't believe he said that to Patrick," Zoe said. "He doesn't always think before he speaks."

"It's okay." Emma fiddled with her croissant, avoiding her sister's eyes.

"Clearly, it's not," Zoe said, her tone gentle. "Want to talk about it?"

"I shouldn't be upset," Emma said, hesitating to say anything. But if she couldn't talk to her sister, who could she talk to? "It's only been two years. Not even. But I felt like he was avoiding the conversation after, and I'm just feeling unsettled."

"You think you might have different ideas about what the future holds?"

"Maybe. And that scares me."

"I get it. After your childhood, any uncertainty probably seems scary," Zoe said. "I did the same to JJ, when I pushed him away for months. After growing up feeling like I wasn't worthy of love, with a mother who couldn't show emotion, JJ's puppy-dog energy was a lot. I still feel bad about how I treated him for months. He was always very clear about his feelings and intentions, and I was difficult. To put it nicely."

"Difficult is one word for it," Emma said, smiling at her sister.

"But I don't see that in Patrick," Zoe said. "He seems incredibly devoted to you. I can't imagine that you aren't on the same page. Can I tell you what I think?"

"Of course," Emma said, surprised her sister had to ask.

"Last year, you were a little out of sorts around Christmas," Zoe said. "You might not remember it, but I do. We all credited it to what had happened with the break-in, and how scared everyone was. But you were quiet and withdrawn, and it's not like you. I saw it start back up a week or so ago, and it got me thinking. I wonder if this has more to do with your mom than with Patrick."

"What do you mean?"

"I think you miss her. I know you miss her," Zoe said, correcting herself when Emma started to speak. "But I also worry that you didn't really get a chance to grieve for her properly. You were just a kid, and you were suddenly thrown into the foster system. You lost me and your mom, and all your stability. It's normal to go into survival mode and squash any emotion. But when the holidays come up, a time when you and she really had amazing memories, it tries to sneak up on you. And your instinct is to shut it down, rather than deal with it."

Emma swallowed hard, considering her sister's words. She let the idea settle around her heart, cause a lump in her throat, before she nodded. "You're probably right," she said. "And everything with Stella the last few months added to it."

"You were worried about losing her," Zoe said.

"Of course. She's been like a mom to me since I moved here," Emma said. "That first day, when I had to meet Patrick's family, she made me feel welcome. And she checked on me all the time over those first few months, to make sure I was okay. It wasn't just Patrick she was caring about, and I knew that. She's made me feel like I belong here."

"I hope I've done the same," Zoe said.

"Of course," Emma replied. "And I would have stayed here no matter what, to be with you. But when I was worried that people thought I was wrong for Patrick, she reassured me that I was the right woman for him. And when I thought my father had come and ruined everything, she was one of the first people to make me feel like I wouldn't be judged for what he did."

"Seeing her so sick was hard on me, never mind how you must have been feeling since you're so close," Zoe said. "I'm sorry I didn't see it at the time. I should have seen you were struggling."

"You had bigger things going on," Emma said, gesturing to her sister's stomach. "Growing me a niece or nephew to spoil. And speaking of, have you told your mother yet?"

"No," Zoe said with a sigh. "I need to. She's been calling for the last few weeks, wanting to come for a visit. I guess I'll need to talk to her."

"She's tried," Emma said. "I know it's hard to forgive her, but she really has been making an effort. On her last visit, we even had a full conversation. And I do believe her apology was real, when we finally talked about the past."

"I hope so," Zoe said. "Otherwise, how do I let her into her grandchild's life?"

"It's Christmas time," Emma said. "Miracles happen this time of year. Give her a chance, and see what happens."

"What are you hoping for this year?" Zoe asked. "I'm sure anything you want, Patrick will get it for you?"

Emma shrugged, not entirely sure how to answer the question. "I don't need anything from him, really," she said. "He's always thoughtful with gifts, so he'll come up with something great."

"And what do you get the man who has everything?" Zoe asked.

"I was thinking about that," Emma said. "We've had a lot of successful rescues come through here over the last two years. Horses, dogs, and goats mainly, but even some others. I'd like to make him a book with pictures of them all when they arrived and when they left, and where they ended up. I started reaching out to the new owners to ask for updates and pictures."

"That's a great idea," Zoe said. "He'll love it."

"You don't think it's too much about me, do you?"

"No," Zoe said. "It's something you've done together. You dedicate more time to it now, just because you can, but he loves it just as much."

"Okay, good," Emma said. "Because I have no other ideas. What are you getting for JJ?"

"A baby," Zoe said with a laugh. "I plan to get him all gifts around being a dad. He'll love it."

"I'm sure he will. I still can't believe you are going to be a mom," Emma said, her eyes misting over. "You're going to be so good."

"I hope you're right," Zoe said. "Thankfully, I'll have JJ there to balance me out."

"Oh, you'll be fantastic," Emma said. "You know what not to do, that's for sure."

Zoe laughed. "True. What about you? Have you and Patrick talked about it at all?"

"What? Having kids?"

"Any of it," Zoe said. "Marriage, kids. The future."

"We both want kids," Emma answered. "We have talked about that a lot. But nothing else."

"Are you ready to start thinking about it? You've been together for a while now."

"We have, but I don't want to pressure him," Emma said.

"I feel like there's more to it that you aren't telling me," Zoe said.

"No," Emma said quickly.

"I won't psychoanalyze you again," Zoe said. "But promise you'll talk to him about some of this. Your mom, your feelings about Stella, maybe even about this."

"I will," Emma said. "When he's not under so much pressure. I promise."

"You matter too," Zoe said softly. "Just because he's a big celebrity doesn't mean you matter less."

"I know," Emma said. "Everything is fine, I promise. Now, let's get online and do some shopping. I'm hoping to get the kids covered today, and Calle has quite the long list to shop for."

***

After a few hours spent shopping individually on their phones and showing each other things on the laptop, Emma needed a break. "I can't believe how late it is. Let me make us a late lunch," she said to Zoe as she stood up from the couch. "You relax."

"Are you sure? I should help." Zoe said it but made no effort to move from where she was settled, with her legs up on the sofa.

"Absolutely," Emma said. "I have more than enough leftovers from yesterday, so you already did the work."

Emma was grabbing bottled water from the fridge when she heard Zoe gasp, and the sound caused a bottle to slip from her hand as she spun around. "Are you okay? Is it the baby?"

Zoe slammed her phone down on the cushion next to her and shook her head. "It's nothing, sorry. I didn't mean to scare you."

"It's something," Emma said. "You just sounded like you saw the world was ending. Tell me what it was."

"I don't want to," Zoe said, a guilty look on her face. "It would ruin your day, and we're having so much fun."

"I'll see it anyway," Emma said, a sense of dread settling in her stomach. The comments about her had been brutal in recent weeks, ever since a reporter had written about her 'Cinderella story'. According to the reporter, Emma had been homeless and poverty-stricken when she had set her sights on Patrick. Being the kind person that he was, he had no idea that she was only with him for his money, and this reporter was determined to save him. Unlike the original Cinderella, apparently Emma did not deserve a happily ever after, at least according to one person. And all the people who added their two cents in the comment section when the article was posted online.

Zoe held the phone close to her chest for a moment before sighing and offering it to her. Emma took it, the dread turning to dismay as she saw the pictures and headline. HOLIDAY HEARTBREAK screamed across the top of the page, above a picture of Patrick. He was getting into a car at the airport, head down and face partially covered by a hat. He looked tired, not heartbroken, Emma thought passively as she scrolled. The article claimed that Patrick had fled his home in Vermont to escape her and was in California to recuperate. Halfway down the page, another picture appeared, this time of Patrick and Nat. They were sitting together in the backseat of the black SUV, racing away from the airport. The caption below claimed that Patrick had turned to former lover Natalie Cloud to recover from betrayal at Emma's hands.

Emma sighed and handed the phone back to Zoe. "They didn't even say why we broke up this time, did they? It's like they think if they keep saying it enough, they can make it happen."

"You can see that Liam is in the car with them," Zoe said, holding the picture up. "They tried to crop him out, but you can see him behind Patrick when he's getting in the car, and it looks like he sat in the passenger seat. They conveniently don't mention that, or that Zane is also in California for the same reason."

"It doesn't matter," Emma said. "I don't know how to make this stop. I just want to live my life and be happy with him, but when will they leave us alone? I don't know how much more of this I can take."

Zoe stood and hugged her, letting Emma cry all over her. The weight of missing her mother, being away from Patrick, and the public scrutiny was just too much to bear. All she had wanted was a nice day with her sister, kicking off the holiday season, and now she couldn't push the darker thoughts from her head. Maybe it would be better to ignore Christmas entirely, rather than pretend that this fantasy life she was living would last forever.

Chapter 5

"I need your help with something," Patrick Burrows had his phone on speaker as he sat in a chair on his patio. The weather in California was drastically different from his home in Vermont, and he wanted to enjoy it for a few minutes. The week in Los Angeles had flown by, his days full of costume alterations, voiceovers and interviews. The schedule had been brutal, but Dan had pulled through and made sure that he would be on his way home as promised. The week had felt endless, and Emma had seemed distant on the phone. He was anxious to get home and get back to normal and kick off their holiday season right.

"What do you need?" Sean, his personal assistant, said through the phone, crisp and efficient.

"This has to stay between us," Patrick said. "I know I can count on your discretion."

"Absolutely," Sean said. "I know where my paycheck comes from."

"And I need whoever you get for me to do the same," Patrick said. "I can ask Dan to draw up an NDA, but I'd rather tell him about this face to face."

"I have a generic one that he sent me," Sean replied. "That's not a problem."

"Great, thanks," Patrick said. He took a deep breath, knowing once he put this out into the universe, it was real. "I want to propose to Emma. I need a ring."

"Not a problem. I'll have someone come to you this afternoon," Sean said. "And congratulations, by the way."

"Thank you," Patrick replied. "Should I go to the jewelry store? I don't want to be ridiculous."

"Well, if you go there, they'll have to shut the store down," Sean said. "And that means there is a higher chance of the news getting out. Someone would need to drive you there, and then people would ask about why it was closed. Not to mention that you have the paparazzi following you everywhere you go. I haven't had a minute of quiet all week, with everyone in town trying to get the inside scoop on where you'll be each night."

"Good point about the trouble it could cause," Patrick said. "And I'm sorry this week has been hard. I can't believe the lies they put out there. What's next? Emma is secretly my sister?"

"Don't even put that out in the universe," Sean said with a groan. "Next thing you know, I'll be fielding calls about that. But it's my job, and I just get to direct them to your public relations firm, so it's not a problem. Regarding the ring, it's well past the time for you to take advantage of what your fame has to offer. Your friends have none of the same hesitation that you have. Take a piece of advice from them."

"Do you talk to their assistants about us?" Patrick thought of his three best friends in the industry. Liam and Natalie had recently decided to settle down near him in Vermont, but Zane was still living the high life. Of the four of them, Zane was the most comfortable in the spotlight, although Liam was a close second. They had spent years traveling the world as a pack, and trusted each other more than anyone else in Hollywood. When Patrick had opted to settle in his small hometown, the last thing he had expected was for two of the three to do the same. But he had no complaints, because he loved having them nearby.

"We do," Sean answered. "It's like a support group. I can't tell you what Zane is up to right now, because I don't want to spoil your fun when you hear. But trust me when I say that you're asking for a jeweler is nothing."

"You always come through for me," Patrick said. "I know I don't make it easy, living in Vermont."

"And yet no one has a problem jumping on a plane to come to you, including me," Sean said. "I get to enjoy the scenery without having to live there. And it helps that you're the nicest guy in Hollywood."

"Far from that," Patrick said with a laugh.

"Oh, you're also the most modest," Sean said. "Let me make a call. I'll have someone there within a few hours. And congratulations."

"She hasn't said yes yet," Patrick said.

"As if anyone would say no to you," Sean replied. "Sexiest man alive twice, don't forget."

Patrick laughed and said goodbye before hanging up and putting the phone down next to him. As if she knew he was talking about her, the phone rang instantly, showing Emma's beautiful face on the screen. He had taken the picture when she was on her horse, and she was radiating happiness.

"Hello, my love," he said. "How are you?"

"Lonely," she said. "I miss you. When are you coming home?"

"Tonight, or tomorrow, I promise," he said. "I'm just waiting for them to tell me I'm all done. But the director seemed confident that I was."

"Do you want me to look at flights for you?"

"No, thanks," he said. "I am taking the studio up on its offer of the plane. Nat and Liam are coming back too, so it makes more sense for the three of us to fly private. All of us going through the airport would cause more problems than it's worth."

"Plus, it will get you home faster," Emma said. "I can't wait to see you."

"Same," he said. "I feel like I've been gone a month."

"If it had been, I would have come with you," she said. "I can't be away from you for that long. But I've been staying busy, so it has gone by fast. I had dinner with your family last night, that was fun. And Holly and I have been keeping each other company since she's been missing Liam. Mike even showed up one day wanting us to work out."

Patrick laughed. "He must be going crazy with Natalie away. And Holly will be glad to have Liam back. At least for five minutes before he starts being annoying."

"Oh, she loves him," Emma said. "There's no chance of her being sick of him. I almost think he's going to propose soon."

"What makes you say that?"

"Something Mike said," Emma responded. "It seemed like maybe he and Liam had talked about it, not wanting to step on the other's toes."

"Huh," Patrick said. "What does it mean that I wasn't included in that?"

"Would you want to be?"

"I guess not," he said. Emma sighed with what sounded like disappointment, so he quickly added on. "I just don't care about doing it at the same time as them. Don't forget, my brothers shared a wedding day. I come from the same cloth."

"Oh," Emma said, smiling at him through the screen. "That's true. But if our day comes, I'd like it to be just us."

"Like run away to an island and elope, just the two of us on a beach?"

"Not that alone," she said. "But small. Private."

"You know that will be hard, right?"

"I know," she said. "I just don't want it to turn into a circus. I know everyone around the world is judging me and thinking I'm not good enough for you."

"Hey," he said softly, wishing he could hold her. "That's not true at all. If anything, I'm the one who's not good enough."

"Yeah, right," she said. "You're more than. You have everything, and I was basically a homeless orphan when you met me. The stories have been running wild all week, so it's never far from mind."

"I'm sorry they've been so hard on you lately. I asked the PR firm to look into it, and see if we can do something to make it stop. You're so much more than what they are saying," he said. "You were searching for your sister, and look at all you found. Now you have a family, a somewhat decent boyfriend, and a horse. What more could you want?"

She looked like she was on the verge of saying something when the doorbell rang on her end of the phone. "I have to go," she said. "I'm having all the girls over tonight."

"Have fun," he said. "I love you. I'll hopefully be home in the morning when you wake up. I'll let you know."

"Can we get our Christmas tree the day you come home? I don't mind waiting for you, but it's so un-Merry in here, we need to fix that."

"Absolutely," he promised. "I'll borrow Jake's truck, and we can go."

"Okay, love you," she said. She blew a kiss and then disconnected, leaving him feeling lonely. He missed her so much when he was away, but on these short, work-heavy trips, it made more sense for her to stay home. In California, she would have been lonely and had nothing to do. At least in Vermont, she had her friends and his family.

Before he could start dwelling on his urgency to get home, his own doorbell rang. He pulled up the app to see who it was before his house manager opened the door but wasn't quick enough. However, the voice coming towards him was unmistakable.

"Hey," Liam called out. "I love this house, but you're so far away from me now."

"That was the point," Patrick said, teasing his friend.

"Now I have to move here," Liam said. "Holly is already talking about it. She wants to be closer to Emma when we're here to shoot the next one."

"I can't believe you're already thinking ahead to the one after this," Patrick said. They were due to leave to shoot a movie in a few weeks, but already had the time blocked on their schedules for the next in the series. Are we going to be here or on location? I thought I heard something about being overseas again," Patrick asked.

"For part of it," Liam said. "We're going to be back in Scotland, which is cool. Bring me back to my roots."

"For part of it," Liam said. "We're going to be in Scotland, which is cool. Bring me back to my roots."

"I thought you were Irish?"

"Close enough," Liam said. "But Zane likes to claim Ireland, so I have to watch myself."

"Well, he has the accent," Patrick pointed out. "You just have the grandparents."

"True," Liam said. "But I could fake the accent. I used to, because I saw how the ladies reacted."

"And now you have Holly," Patrick said. "Speaking of, I just found out from Emma that you and Mike are in a race to propose?"

"Wow, word spreads fast," Liam said. "We talked about it. I don't want to rain on his parade or have Holly feeling like she needs to share the spotlight."

"I don't think she would mind," Patrick said.

"With Nat? The biggest female movie star in the world? The woman men dream about?"

"I didn't think of that," Patrick said. "That could be a problem."

"I think Mike should do what JJ did," Liam said. He was referencing their friend, who proposed to his wife and got married the same night in Las Vegas. "Don't let the paparazzi even know she's engaged. Or better yet, don't even let the world know she's married. Speaking of, my agent told me not to do it."

"Not to propose?"

"Or even get married," Liam said. "And if I do, she wants me to keep it under wraps."

"Why? I would think pictures of your wedding alone could net her a huge deal," Patrick said.

"She said part of my appeal is the single bad boy," Liam said. "They would rather Holly stay hidden in Vermont."

"That's terrible," Patrick said. "How does Holly feel about that?"

"She doesn't mind," Liam said. "She likes to work, and said if her face was all over magazines, it would make that harder. She likes to be able to sneak in through the back door of events and not have to worry."

"I love to show Emma off, but the press lately has been brutal," Patrick said.

"For you? That's weird," Liam said. "They normally love you."

"They still do," Patrick said. "It's Emma they go after. I probably should have done what you do, kept her to myself."

"You have a different public image," Liam pointed out. "Zane and I were the wild bachelors. You were always the one people dreamed of marrying and having babies with. It was normal to share that with the world when you found what you were looking for."

"True," Patrick said.

"So, what's up? Are we ready to go home yet? Holly is going nuts about all the holiday things we need to do," Liam said. "Not only is it Christmas, which she loves, but it's her birthday. It's her favorite time of the year, and it's when we first connected. To think we just met last year at this time is crazy."

Patrick scratched his chin, debating whether to tell his friend about the ring and his plan to propose. He knew Liam would be excited for him, but anyone who knew added to the risk of the news getting out. Better to keep it to himself for now.

"You look like you're trying to find a way to create world peace over there," Liam said. "What's going on?"

Patrick's house manager, Mary, interrupted them with a tray of coffee and fruit. Liam grinned at her as she put it down. "Is Patrick still watching his weight? I was hoping for one of your amazing cookies."

"I'll go get you some," Mary said. "And Mr. Patrick is perfect just as he is. But he mentioned earlier that he might be flying tonight, so I thought a hydrating snack would be better."

"You're always so wise, Mary," Liam said, reaching for her hand. "Will you please quit on him and come manage my house? I promise my undying love and devotion, and more money."

"I would never leave him," Mary said, winking at Patrick. "Even when he moved out to the boonies, it never crossed my mind."

"See!" Liam cried, looking at Patrick. "We need to get you back to the beach."

"No, no," Mary said quickly. "I like it here. It's quieter. And Miss Emma is happier here."

"She is," Patrick said. "And Liam will like it when he moves."

"Fine," Liam said with a sigh. "I'll get someone working on that. It will be a nice surprise for Holly."

"You don't think she would want to be involved in picking the house?" Patrick asked.

"I don't think she'll mind," Lian answered, looking thoughtful. "But that's a good point. I'll feel her out. She moved so much when she worked as a travel nurse, she said she can live anywhere. I think if we can find something close to here, she'll be thrilled. And it's not like we can't change whatever about the house she doesn't like."

"True," Patrick said. "You'll have just finished the construction in Vermont in time to start here."

"What a project that was," Liam said. "I'm glad the youth center was rebuilt so quickly. As much as I liked having them there, it was a lot of noise and activity. And we couldn't start renovations on the house until they moved."

"It was nice of you to host them for so long," Patrick said. "No one would have expected that of you."

"Don't tell anyone," Liam said with a laugh. "Another thing that would ruin the image. Liam Dorsey offering his house and property to be used as a youth center is not something the public sees me doing."

"It must get exhausting," Patrick said.

"What?"

"Having to play a character all the time," he said. "You can never just be yourself."

"I am," Liam replied. "When I'm with you guys, or Holly. I can be myself in Vermont, no one is looking to sell me out there. It's nice, really. Being able to be a part of a community and not worry about it."

"It is," Patrick said. The second-best decision he had made was moving back to Windsor Peak. The first was falling in love with Emma, which he couldn't even take credit for. His heart had done all the work there, and now he just needed to find a way to make it permanent.

Chapter 6

Emma opened the door for her sister, Zoe, who was carrying two large bags. "Oh, Zoe, you should have called me to come out," she cried. "Let me take those. You shouldn't be carrying heavy stuff."

"You sound like JJ," Zoe said. "I'm pregnant, not incapacitated."

"You still need to be careful," Emma said. "It's icy, and you're carrying precious cargo."

"I know," Zoe said, hugging her quickly once they were inside. "Trust me. After having a miscarriage, I was over the top afraid when I got this positive test. But this little bean is doing great."

"I'm so glad," Emma said, feeling tears gather. "I can't wait to be an aunt. I'm going to be the best one in the world."

"Don't let Finley hear you say that," Zoe cautioned her. JJ's sister Finley had become a close friend and would share the aunt duties when the baby was born. "She had a quick moment of declaring herself the world's best aunt, when her brothers had to co-uncle. I took the wind out of her sails a little when I reminded her that I also have a sister."

"Can't we share the title?" Emma asked.

"That's fine," Zoe said. "As long as you don't fight over it."

"She has bigger things to think about," Emma said. "I can't wait until she gets here so I can see the ring. Is she glowing?"

"Yes," Zoe said. "Happiest I've ever seen her. She and Evan went through the wringer, and I'm so glad they came out the other side. JJ was bursting at the seams knowing he was going to propose. That man cannot keep a secret. It's shocking to me that he can be the town sheriff and not be spilling all the hot gossip."

"Seriously," Emma said with a laugh. "He keeps all the good stuff from us."

The doorbell rang, and Emma rushed to open it. It was cold outside, winter finally settled in to stay in Vermont. With the wind chill, it was below zero, and she didn't want her friends to be stuck outside. When she pulled the door open, she found Holly along with Shea and Kendra. Kendra and Shea were neighbors, and they had obviously swung by to pick up Shea's sister on the way.

"Hi," she said, pulling the door open wider. "Come in. I have a fire going to warm you up."

"You forget that we're all native to Windsor Peak," Shea said with a laugh as she passed by. "This is nothing. Wait until February."

"I know," Emma said, shivering. "I just try to pretend it's not coming again. Wasn't last year enough?"

"You're Canadian," Zoe pointed out. "How are you not used to this?"

"I agree," Holly said. "I had always chosen nursing assignments in warm climates before I moved here and I've adjusted."

"I don't know," Emma said. "Maybe all those years of not being warm have caught up with me."

"Well, if you're going to play that card," Holly said, teasing her. "I can't compete with sleeping in a freezing barn."

The doorbell rang again, and Emma clapped her hands. "That must be Finley," she cried, rushing to the door.

Finley was smiling when the door opened, looking like the weather didn't bother her in the slightest. "Thanks for inviting me," she said.

"Of course," Emma said, waving her in. "We're so excited to celebrate with you. Is Evan okay with it being a girl's night?"

"Is Evan okay being home alone with a book and his dog?" Finley asked. "That's like asking if it's cold outside. He's more than fine."

"Come in," Emma said. "Take off your coat and gloves so we can ogle the ring."

Finley laughed but pulled them off and held up her left hand for the other women to admire. They gushed over it for several minutes before settling in by the fire to hear about the proposal. As she talked, Emma couldn't help but think about Patrick. They were nearing two years together, and couples around them were getting engaged with far less time. Maybe he wasn't the marrying type? Or wasn't ready to commit to her?

She excused herself as Finley concluded her story, going to the kitchen to grab the champagne she had chilling. Zoe followed her, standing just beside the refrigerator as it opened.

"I got sparkling cider as well," Emma told her sister. "I didn't want anyone to feel left out."

"What was the expression on your face just now?" Zoe asked, accepting the bottle from Emma.

"What do you mean?"

"You looked weird," Zoe said. "Almost sad."

"No, not at all," Emma said. "I'm happy for Finley."

"Me too," Zoe said. "But you can be whatever it is you're feeling too."

"I just…" Emma started to say what she felt, but found she couldn't put it into words without sounding selfish.

"What? You know you can tell me anything."

"It's been a while for us," Emma said. "I don't know what to think."

"You're sad it's not you?"

"Not like that," Emma said. "I don't want to take anything from Finley. It's just that we haven't talked about it at all. I brought it up with him earlier, and he didn't say anything that would make me think he was even considering it. I don't know what to do."

"You could ask him," Zoe said.

"Like propose?" Emma stared at her sister in horror. "Do you know who my boyfriend is? I could never do that."

"Not propose," Zoe said. "Or maybe. But you could just ask him what his thoughts are on marriage."

"We kind of talked about it today," Emma said. "But just in general, about whether he wants to space it out from his friends, and what kind of wedding we would want. I don't want to push him."

"Em," Zoe said softly. "If you can't ask him that, maybe you're not ready? That seems like a basic relationship discussion, to make sure you're on the same page."

"I don't want him to think I'm rushing him," Emma explained. "Or that I'm not happy. Because I am, he's amazing."

"And so are you," Zoe said loyally. "Don't forget that."

They brought the bottles over to where the other women were talking and laughing, forcing herself to push the invasive thoughts away. She loved Patrick, and he loved her. That was enough.

"Are you officially moving in with him?" Shea was asking as they rejoined the others.

"I kind of already was," Finley said, laughing. "But yes. I'll be moving all my stuff over. It's the end of an era for Desmond and I. We've never lived apart, other than two years in college dorms. But as soon as we could, we moved off campus and shared a place."

"It must be nice to have a twin," Kendra said. "I always wished that I were one as a kid. Being an only child is lonely. I wanted a built-in best friend."

"That's pushing it," Finley said with a laugh. "After all, Des is a big personality to deal with every day. He can be exhausting, but he's always there for me. I really did hit the jackpot with siblings. And siblings-in-law."

Zoe reached over and squeezed her hand. "Same," she said. "I never imagined I would ever get married, never mind into a big, loud family. It's the opposite of everything I had as a kid, and I love it."

"I hope so, because I'm about to fill your life with family time," Finley said. "Planning this wedding is going to take a team effort."

"When are you thinking?" Shea asked. "And will you do it here?"

"I happen to know a place that would be happy to host the reception," Kendra said, winking at Finley. Kendra owned the local restaurant, and she and Zoe were co-owners of a store and function space next door.

"I'll keep that in mind," Finley said. "Evan is still working on his relationship with his family, so I'll give them a little time. It will be nice to enjoy being engaged before we rush into the craziness."

"You couldn't be more different from your brother," Zoe said. "JJ did it all in one night."

"You take the credit for that," Emma reminded her. "If you had just admitted that you were even dating him, never mind that you were in love, he wouldn't have had to do that."

"It was romantic, though," Zoe said, blushing slightly. "I can admit that now."

"It sure was," Kendra said. "And you went viral. What more could you ask for?"

"I loved that video," Holly said. "And I didn't even know any of you yet, other than through Shea's descriptions. Then all of a sudden, there's a video blowing up my feed of a guy proposing in front of a whole stadium. Even though the commenters all thought they were strangers, or that it would never happen, I could see that she loved him back. That was amazing."

"No one would have even recorded it if Patrick and Nat weren't there," Zoe pointed out. "You can thank them for that."

"Imagine when you two get engaged," Shea said, pointing at Emma and Holly. "It will be a circus."

Holly shook her head. "Not for us," she said. "No one really even knows we're in a relationship, so we definitely won't be showcasing an engagement."

"That's crazy to me," Kendra said. "How it's kept so quiet."

"Hollywood is a weird place," Emma said. "They can make you whatever they need to. It's a lot of smoke and mirrors out there."

"And Liam needs to be a bachelor playboy," Holly said. "Fortunately, I'm not the jealous type. And I don't pay attention to the gossip magazines."

"You would go crazy if you did," Emma said. "That was the best advice I got from Nat. Ignore it unless you hear it direct from the horse's mouth. Sometimes it's hard for me to see what's true and what's not, and it's my life. Like this week, with the rumors flying that Nat and Patrick ran off together. It's really hard to look the other way, or focus on the truth when all the lies are so loud. Especially when people message me directly, how do I ignore that?"

"You just look over at your incredibly handsome boyfriend, and realize any negativity comes from jealousy," Zoe said. "Anyone that tries to cause you problems has to go through me. Or at least, my husband, because I'll be waddling very soon and would find it difficult to perform my ninja moves."

They all laughed and took glasses to toast Finley. The bride-to-be beamed as they all wished her a lifetime of happiness with her soon-to-be husband, and Emma focused on that rather than the unsettled feeling she had. It was time to take her own advice and wait to see Patrick in person before worrying too much about their future. Zoe was right. She needed to ask him and hear from his own mouth what his thoughts were. All this guessing was just making her crazy.

***

"Do you want me to sleep over with you?" Holly asked as the other women were preparing to leave. "You've been unusually quiet all night. I'm happy to stay if you're feeling lonely or there's something on your mind that you want to talk about."

"No, it's okay," Emma said. "Unless you'd rather not drive, or be alone yourself?"

"I know it gets scary in these big houses when no one else is around," Holly said. "Freaks me out too sometimes."

"Patrick had an elaborate alarm system put in after the break-in," Emma said. "It's impossible to feel anything but safe here."

"You sure?"

"I'll be alright," Emma said. "They might be home tomorrow. Have you heard anything from Liam?"

"He was at Patrick's earlier, waiting to hear from the director," Holly shared. "But he said Patrick got weird and made him leave. And then he wasn't answering him when he was trying to get him to go get something to eat."

"That's weird," Emma said, frowning. "He's not like that. I hope he's not getting sick."

"I'm sure he's fine," Holly said. "Maybe he's just had enough of Liam. I know he can be a lot."

"No, he's not," Emma said with a laugh. "And they're used to being together for long periods of time. He seemed fine when I talked to him earlier."

"Who knows?" Holly said, pulling on her coat. "If you're sure you'll be alright, I'll head home."

"Yes, but thanks," Emma said, hugging her. "You're a good friend."

"So are you," Holly said. "I don't know how I got so lucky to have this life, but I'm so glad."

"Same," Emma said with a smile. "I'll talk to you in the morning. If you hear anything from Liam, will you text me?"

"Absolutely," Holly agreed, pulling open the door. Emma watched her walk to her car, then closed the door and flipped the lock. Although she had been honest with her friend that she felt safe in the house with the security system, the sudden silence still caused a pang. She wasn't scared, she just didn't want to be alone with her thoughts. Reaching for her own heavy jacket, she headed to the kitchen door, which led to the stable.

When she slid open the heavy door, the horses were mostly sleeping. Only her horse, Whiskey, was standing at her gate as if waiting for her. She walked toward the mare, careful not to upset the newer rescues, who were still uncertain of their safety. Patrick had opened up his barn to a local rescue, offering them spots when needed until permanent homes could be found. He had recently added on to the stable, making even more space available. They currently housed a dozen rescues in addition to the six that Patrick owned.

"Hey, girl," Emma said softly as she approached Whiskey. "Are you lonely too?"

The horse nudged her hand, then moved closer so Emma could press her face to its snout. She wrapped her hand in the horse's mane, taking comfort from the solid animal.

"I'm being silly," Emma said to the horse. "I know he loves me. Why is it a big deal to get married? As long as we're together, that's enough. Right?"

The horse blinked her big, brown eyes, unable to answer. Much like Whiskey, Emma had bounced around for years, feeling unwelcome and unloved along the way. And just like the horse, she had found her home with Patrick. Emma needed to trust in Patrick and their love the same way Whiskey trusted her.

Chapter 7

"I don't know what I'm looking for," Patrick said to the man across from him. Victor Guilia was the jeweler to the stars, according to the text from Sean. He had arrived within a few hours of Patrick's phone call to his assistant, carrying briefcases and accompanied by two armed guards. Fortunately, Liam had been easy enough to send away, happy to run home and pack at the possibility of getting on a plane that night.

"Tell me about her," Victor said, leaning back in his chair.

"She's my everything," Patrick said. "She's delicate but strong. Beautiful but not intimidating. She's so caring. She has a bigger heart than anyone I've ever met. She rescues animals, and does that full time now, working with a few different organizations. We always have a full house, from horses to dogs and cats. Even guinea pigs once, and bunnies after Easter."

"What does she wear for jewelry now?"

"Nothing," Patrick said. "Other than a necklace that was her mother's. I've bought her things over the years, and she wears them when we go to events, but every day, she doesn't wear much."

"So, she wouldn't want something elaborate," Victor surmised.

"But I don't want to go too modest," Patrick said quickly. "I feel like it needs to be a representation of how I feel about her."

"Are you proposing at Christmas?" Victor asked.

"I'm not sure," Patrick said. "I need to figure out how to do it. This is just step one."

"A lot of people get engaged over the holidays, and they definitely want the wow factor," Victor explained. "They get caught up in the lights and season and forget that it's something she will wear every day. I'm glad you're being logical."

"I wish I felt like I was," Patrick admitted. "Should I have her involved in this? Asked her what she likes?"

Victor shrugged. "That's very common," he said. "Especially among your peers. But it's also nice to surprise her. Show her that you thought of her when you were apart, and that you know her well enough to choose for her."

"You're right," Patrick said. "And I'm more traditional than most, I think. I'd like to surprise her."

"Let's start with the band," Victor suggested. "Do you have a metal in mind?"

"I don't even know what the options are," Patrick said, laughing.

"Platinum and gold are the two traditional," Victor explained, pulling bands out of one case. "Rose gold is also popular now, it has this pink sheen. With wedding bands for men, we use a lot of titanium and different materials than what we usually do for the engagement rings."

"I like this," Patrick said, touching a rose gold band. "It looks warm, like her."

"Okay, so let's get those options out," Víctor said, smoothly pulling a case out of the bag. "If you don't see something perfect here, we can make it. I have a tablet that I can draw on if that's better."

Patrick picked up each band carefully, studying it from all angles. There was everything from a plain circle to elaborate carved designs, and he was trying to picture each one on Emma's hand. He stopped as he held one that was designed to look like petals and leaves encircling the band, so the central diamond would shine like a flower. "This is pretty," he said.

"We can do diamonds or gemstones in the band in addition to the main one," Vicor explained, pointing to spots on the ring. "But first, let's look at some stones."

A guard stepped forward with a case, placing it on the table and taking the other away, leaving just the one band that Patrick held. Trays of diamonds were pulled out, along with other precious gemstones. It had to be millions of dollars in jewels, sitting on Patrick's dining room table, he realized. He was dying to share this with Emma but couldn't tell her about it without her knowing the reason why it was happening.

"This is just over three carats, and ethically sourced. That's been a big factor for a lot of your peers lately. It costs more, but better for your image, and your manager already asked that all of my inventory today meet those criteria," Victor said, holding a stone in a large pair of tweezers over the ring. "We can go bigger or smaller than this. This one is flawless, with a high score for clarity as well."

"It's stunning," he said, looking carefully at the diamond. "What would you suggest for the other spots?"

Victor pulled a tray closer, showing him smaller diamonds. "These are the same as the main diamond," he said, gesturing to one tray. "Smaller, but equal in clarity and quality. They'll go along the side to fill in the petals."

The jeweler carefully placed the stones in the empty spots, holding the ring so they would stay in place so that Patrick could see what it looked like. He stared in amazement at the ring, overwhelmed at the thought of what it represented. Not only would it be stunning, but it meant his love for Emma was solidified for life. The ring was deceptively simple, yet beautiful when you got closer to it, much like Emma. And much like the flower on the ring, she had bloomed over the last two years, becoming confident in her own skin. She loved those around her fiercely and brought out the best in everyone, especially him.

"That's perfect," he said finally to Victor, who was waiting patiently. "It's exactly what I didn't know I wanted."

"This is it then? You're sure?"

"Positive," Patrick said, nodding. "Am I able to take it with me today? We're flying out in a few hours."

"I can set it right here," Victor assured him. "That's not a problem."

"I'll get my wallet," Patrick said, starting to rise.

"No need," Victor said. "Your assistant already left the payment information with the store. It's all taken care of."

"Great," Patrick said. "You made this very easy on me. I appreciate it."

"If you don't mind me taking a few minutes, I'll get this all set for you," Victor said.

"I'll go grab a cup of coffee and leave you to it," Patrick responded, backing away.

His phone rang as he entered the kitchen, and he saw Natalie's name on the screen. "Hey," he said after clicking to answer. "How's it going?"

"I want to get out of here," she said. "I'm going crazy. I can't do anything without people following me, and I miss Mike. Can we go home now?"

"I think we were just waiting on you," he said. "Liam was here earlier because he was bored, so he's done. I finished all my reshoots and voiceovers and did all my press yesterday. That means I'm done."

"Perfect," she said. "I finished this morning. Want me to call and tell them we can be wheels up in two hours?"

Patrick glanced over to the dining room where Victor was hard at work. As much as he wanted to see Emma, he didn't want to rush the man. "Make it three," he said. "Or tell them two, but you might have to wait on me."

"If that happens, I will make sure to note it on my calendar," she teased him. "It would be the first time that I wasn't the last one to arrive."

Patrick laughed. "Most likely, it will be Liam," he said. "I probably should have kept him here so he couldn't go get into trouble somewhere."

"No," Natalie said. "He's too happy with Holly to do that. He wants to get home."

"It's still funny to me, hearing you call it home," Patrick said. "But I'm so glad you moved there."

"Me too," Natalie said. "If you had told me two years ago that I'd be living in a tiny town in Vermont, and that I would be this happy, I never would have believed you."

"Same," Patrick said. "But everything worked out for both of us. All three of us."

"Now we just need to work on Zane," Natalie said with a laugh. "But that might be impossible."

"I'll see you at the airport," Natalie said. "Unless you want me to pick you up?"

"No," he said quickly, glancing at the jeweler again. "That would be out of your way. I'll get a car."

Victor waved to him from the table, so he quickly ended the call and went to where the man was working. The jeweler showed him the progress so far, the band now half done with the smaller stones, which Patrick nodded his approval for. Half an hour later, he accepted the small ring box and stared at the finished product. It was spectacular, and so perfectly Emma, that he couldn't wait to give it to her.

***

Early the next morning, Emma woke him with a kiss. He had landed late, and although he had tried not to wake her, she had sleepily rolled toward him and put her head on his chest before promptly falling back to sleep. He had immediately followed suit, happy to be back where he belonged.

"Hey, you," she said. "I'm sorry to wake you up, but I'm excited to see you."

"Same," he said. "I missed you."

"Me too," she said. "Although according to the gossip, you were recovering from our breakup, and I was squatting here in your house."

"Why do you read that?"

"I can't seem to avoid it," she said, looking sad. "People send them to me, and it's just everywhere. I wish I could ignore it."

"You've talked to Missy about this," he said, referencing the woman who handled his public relations. "Remember what she told you?"

"Ten percent truth at best," she said. "And to trust my real life, not what the press is saying."

"Is there something in particular that you think is true about this latest bit?"

"No, I'm just being silly. It's the time of year, and I missed you," she said. "I'll put it out of my mind, I promise."

"Are you sure? Mike said there were a bunch of pictures and stories about Nat and I that he laughed off," he said. "Did that bother you?"

"I know how happy Nat and Mike are," she said. "And she's too good a friend to worry about something happening. She wouldn't do that to me."

"Neither would I," he said, feeling hurt and confused at her words.

"Of course, I know that," she said. "I'm sorry, I didn't mean it like that. I just meant it would have been different if it were someone I didn't know."

"I don't like that you would feel insecure in any way," he said. "Are things worse than usual?"

"No, I think it's just the time of year," she said. "I've been thinking about my mom a lot. Zoe pointed out that I was sad last year too, so I'm trying to figure out how best to deal with the emotions. It just didn't help that you were so far away."

"I'm sorry."

"Nothing to be sorry for," she said. "I know you didn't have any control over the schedule. You're back now, and I already feel better. And if you remember, you promised me a Christmas tree today."

"Oh, did I?" he asked, rolling to make it so that she was lying across his chest. "What if I changed my mind and wanted to spend the whole day here?"

She met his eyes with a raised eyebrow. "What if I promise some special time under the tree later?"

"I'm a little afraid of where sap could go," he said. "But I'm game."

She laughed and started to move off him. "Okay, in front of the fire while the tree glows beside us. Better?"

"Anywhere with you is where I want to be," he said. He stood and stretched next to the bed. "I'm going to take a quick shower."

"I'll go make coffee," she replied, pulling on a robe. "Then maybe I'll join you, so don't be too quick."

***

Two hours later, they were bundled up and walking the tree lot at a neighboring farm. It offered fresh-cut trees lined up by the barn, or you could opt to go into the field and cut your own down. Patrick glanced over at Emma as they walked. "Are we taking one that's already cut? Or going old school and testing my lumberjack skills?"

"As much as the idea of watching you chop down a tree intrigues me," she said. "Let's take a look at these first. I want it to be perfect."

"We probably should have special ordered," Patrick said. "I'm realizing now that we might need something bigger than what they would have. Or than would fit into the truck."

"No," Emma said, shaking her head. "We don't need a Hollywood tree. These will be fine."

They walked through the rows of trees, Emma examining each one. As they went, neighbors stopped them to say hello, slowing them down. It made him happy that the Windsor Peak residents greeted Emma warmly and genuinely wanted to talk to her. It was so different from when they were in California, and she was ignored by anyone who wanted something from him.

Patrick felt for the ring box in his pocket, glancing around at the crowd. It was too public to propose here, and his brother had already done a proposal at the same place. It would be better to wait until they were at home, alone, before he popped the question. It felt like the box was burning a hole in his pocket, and he was desperate to present her with it, but he needed it to be perfect. She deserved that. Any ideas he had about waiting until Christmas morning to present her with it had flown away the moment he had seen the ring. All he wanted now was to see it on her finger and know what it represented for their future.

"Uncle Patty!" He heard the cry seconds before he was slammed into from behind, little arms wrapping around his legs. "You came home!"

Patrick turned and scooped up Calle, the eight-year-old ball of energy that was his niece. She was almost getting too big to pick up, but he was happy to still be able to do it and get her big hug. Dan and Kendra trailed behind Calle, along with a stroller containing a bundle that had to be his nephew Declan.

"I missed you," he said to Calle as he put her back down. "How is school?"

"Boring," she said with an eye roll. "And the boys are so annoying."

"Good," he said, meeting Dan's eyes. "Keep it that way."

"What does that mean?" Calle asked, hands on her hips.

"Never date," Patrick told her. "No one will ever be good enough for you."

"Are you good enough for Emma?" Calle challenged him. "And when can I start calling her Auntie Emma? I call Auntie Shea that, but I can't Emma? It's confusing."

"It is," he agreed, stifling a laugh. "I'm sure Emma wouldn't mind if you called her that."

"Not until you put a ring on it," Dan said. "That's what we told her. And she has high hopes for being a flower girl, not that I'm pressuring you."

Emma laughed from behind him, and he turned to see that her cheeks had turned pink. Whether it was embarrassment or the cold, he wasn't sure. "No pressure," she said. "But Calle would make a very pretty flower girl."

"I got to do it at my mom and dad's wedding," Calle told Emma. "Uncle Jake and Aunt Shea got married at the same time. I wonder why you didn't?"

"Well, we didn't know each other yet," Emma said. "So that would have been a little weird."

Calle scrunched up her face as if deep in thought before nodding. "Okay, but now you do. Right?"

Patrick glanced over where Dan and Kendra were laughing, seeing they would be no help. Thankfully, his Jake and Shea were coming in behind them, pulling everyone's attention away from the subject at hand. Charlie was carrying his baby sister, Isobel, who was wide-eyed and staring at all the bright lights around the tree lot.

"Welcome home," Charlie said, hugging Patrick quickly.

Shea and Jake followed suit, and Patrick kissed Izzie on the head before fist-bumping Charlie. Jake held the leash for his service dog, Rex, but Patrick resisted the urge to pet him since he was on duty.

"Did you all plan this?" Patrick asked, glancing between his brothers and sisters-in-law.

"Emma mentioned you were coming," Shea said. "We thought it would be fun to do the same."

"I might have texted them when we left the house," Emma said. "We thought you would want to see everyone."

"I do," Patrick said. "I was going to text to see if everyone wanted to come to dinner tomorrow night?"

"Sure," Jake said. "You cooking?"

Patrick laughed. "I'll spare you all that," he said. "I figured I could text Zoe and get some trays."

"Perfect," Kendra said. "My bottom line appreciates that most of your meals come from the business."

"We're going to go now," Patrick said, steering Emma away. "We'll see you tomorrow."

"I thought you would be happy to see them," Emma whispered as they walked away.

"I am," Patrick replied. "But I'm cold. And I want to enjoy this with just you, to kick off our Christmas season together. Let's find a tree and get home, and we'll catch up with them tomorrow."

***

Emma turned on the Christmas music when they arrived at home, then helped Patrick carry the tree in. After a lot of laughter, they wrangled the gigantic tree and got it standing straight up.

"I think it's going to fall," Emma said, staring at it with concern.

"Should we tie it to the wall?" Patrick studied it, considering how he could anchor it.

"No, it should be okay," Emma replied. "I hope."

They pulled out boxes of decorations, including the new lights that Emma had ordered, and got to work. He was singing along with Silent Night when Emma stopped working to stare at him.

"What?"

"It's intimidating," she said.

"What is?"

"Your voice," she replied. "I was just about to start singing and then heard you. It's hard to date someone so perfect."

"I am not," Patrick objected. "You of all people know that."

"Pretty close," Emma said. "Not that I'm complaining. I just realized I can't sing along without ruining it."

"You could never," Patrick said. "As a matter of fact, you make everything better. My life is brighter and happier with you in it."

She smiled at him and kissed him lightly. "I love you too," she said. "And I really didn't mean anything bad by that. You know how much you've changed my life."

The song switched to one by Ed Sheeran, which Patrick knew was one of Emma's favorites. They had danced in the kitchen to it as Ed sang about doing exactly that, and now when Patrick heard the song, he thought of her. Of all they had overcome to be together, of the pain they had left behind and what they had to look forward to. She was on the other side of the tree, looking up at it, but he could see her lips moving along with the song. Before he could give it any more thought, he dropped to a knee and waited for her to see him.

Chapter 8

"We did a good job," Emma said, circling the tree slowly. "I think our ornament to branch ratio is perfect."

When Patrick didn't reply, she looked for him, not seeing him at her first glance. When she heard his voice singing a line from the song, which he often quoted to her, she gasped. He was on one knee, gazing at her with so much love in his eyes.

"Emma Martin," he said as she approached him. He took her hand when she got close enough but stayed where he was. "I love you. So much that it hurts. You're everything I never knew that I needed. You make me feel safe, and like I can be myself all the time. We've built this home together, but I know I could be anywhere with you, and it would feel like home. I want to be yours and know that you're mine forever. I want to have babies who look just like you. I want to grow old with you, and battle through all that life throws at us. Will you please do me the ultimate honor and say you'll marry me?"

He opened a ring box, and she gasped at the glow of the diamond inside. It was hard to see anything through the tears that were falling freely, and she couldn't speak to even say the words. She nodded, laughing and swiping at the tears. "Yes," she said. "Yes, Patrick. I love you, and there's nothing I want more than to spend my life with you."

He caught her as she threw herself at him, as she knew he would. There had been so much fear and uncertainty in her past, and this man had made her feel safe and whole. Knowing she would be this happy forever was almost overwhelming, but she knew this would be remembered as one of the best moments of her life. After she had thoroughly kissed him, he pulled back and reached for her left hand, sliding the ring on. It fit perfectly, and she gasped at the sight of it. It looked like a flower on her finger, delicate but powerful, and almost glowed with warmth. It was perfect.

"I had this made for you," Patrick said. "But if you don't like it, we can go together and he can do a new one. I won't be upset."

"Patrick, it's perfect," she said. "I can't believe how gorgeous it is. I'm almost afraid to lose it."

"It's insured," he said with a smile. "No one was letting me get on a plane with that in my pocket and not having that taken care of. Sean had already sent the paperwork to the insurance company before I even arrived at the airport."

"Of course he did," she said with a grin. "Did he get to see it first?"

"No, the only person who saw it before you was Mary," he said. "She was home when I had it made. You wouldn't believe how it happened, so I have to tell you all about it. But for now, should we call Zoe and tell her the news? Or do you want to invite them over for dinner tomorrow night, with my family, and we can surprise them all at once?"

"Let's do that," Emma said. "I feel like this is a dream, so I need a little time to wrap my head around it before the chaos begins."

"Speaking of," Patrick said, looking uncertain suddenly.

"What?"

"Missy was suggesting that we try to keep this on the down low for now," he said. "Especially after all the attention over the last few weeks. The press will run a story claiming that this is confirmation that we were having problems, and one of us is desperate to stay together. I don't want any negativity in our lives right now. I'd rather just enjoy the next few weeks with you and let everything settle down. After the holidays, we can figure out how to announce it."

"I'm fine with keeping it quiet," she said. "That sounds better that having the press descend on Windsor Peak, ruining the holidays."

He looked relieved as he smiled. "Good," he said. "We'll have to talk about what kind of wedding we want."

"I don't care, as long as you're waiting for me at the altar," she promised him. "Anything else is just extra. We could go to town hall on Monday, and I'd be happy."

***

By the next afternoon, Emma and Patrick had thoroughly decorated for the holiday. It seemed like every inch of the house was covered in Christmas decorations, Emma realized as she glanced around. The tree was gigantic next to the fire, resplendent in lights and ornaments. Clear glass snowflakes that she had found at the Harvest Festival were hanging on the tree and in the windows, as well in some strategic spots where they reflected the lights. Patrick had gotten the ladder out and hung wreaths along the windows in front and then helped her secure a garland on the mantel and the banister along the stairs. It was finally feeling merry inside, and between the decor and the ring on her finger, Emma was giddy.

"It looks amazing in here," Patrick said, hugging her from behind. "You did good work."

"You too," she said. "Thank you for making everything so perfect for us."

"Speaking of," he said, taking her hand and leading her to the couch. Once they were settled down next to each other, she turned to face him and waited for him to continue. "We should talk a little about what we both want for the wedding, before everyone else gets here and puts in their opinions."

"I meant what I said," she replied. "I would marry you anywhere."

"Okay," he said with a laugh. "I feel the same. But I also want you to have the perfect day. I had some thoughts on it."

"Lay them on me."

"We could go to an island," he said. "Sean already sent me options from a resort on a private island in the Fiji area. We could have the entire island, with those bungalows over the ocean."

"That sounds amazing," she said. "But far away. And we have several people who are pregnant who will want to come, and the travel would be too much on them. And the kids."

"True," Patrick replied. "Even if we all flew private, it would be hard. Option two, according to Sean, would be perfect to give you a day a princess deserves."

"I'm intrigued," she said.

"We could rent out Disney World," he said. "Or at least, the Magic Kingdom. Apparently, there is a clause in my movie contract that gives me the ability to request a stay each year in Cinderella's castle, which I have never done. But we could stay in the castle and get married right there."

"Wow," Emma said. "I've never even been, but that sounds amazing."

"Really?" Patrick perked up. "I can have Sean make some calls and get more details. He also has about fifteen other beach locations for us to consider."

"When are you thinking?"

"Good question," Patrick said. "We leave in January for the movie, so I guess after that?"

"That's at least six months away, if not longer," Emma said. She felt her good spirits disappearing quickly at the thought of waiting that long.

"We can do it before, if you'd rather? I just don't want to rush you."

"We have six weeks before we leave, right? And four weeks until Christmas," Emma said thoughtfully. "I don't think we need that long to plan. Let's put Sean to the test, see if he could make it happen so we could all be back in Windsor Peak for Christmas. Worst case, we settle on something in the spring and have that to look forward to."

"But ideally, you'd like to get married in the next three weeks?"

"Yes," she said, feeling more certain. "All I want is to be your wife. I don't need a lot of fuss, I just want us to be able to declare our love and commitment to each other. Can we see if it's a possibility?"

"Of course," he said, standing up. "I'm going to go into my office and call him. Let me know when people start arriving."

***

The doorbell rang a short while later, pulling Emma away from staring at the ring on her finger. She realized as she walked to open it that they hadn't made a plan on how to share the news. Since he didn't come out of his office to greet his family, she stuck her hand in her pocket to hide. As the door swung open, she saw it was Zoe and JJ. He was carrying massive trays from Zoe's catering business, which he brought to the kitchen before kissing Emma on the cheek.

"One more load from the car," he said, heading back out the door.

"He won't let me carry anything," Zoe said with an eye roll.

"Well, you're pregnant and he loves you," Emma said, hugging her sister. "I can't believe how you're starting to pop."

"I had to wear leggings today because nothing with a button will fit," Zoe said. "I think it makes it more pronounced than when I was wearing regular clothes. Plus, this sweater isn't as bulky as what I've been wearing for weeks. But I guess it's time to shop for maternity clothes."

"Oh, that's so exciting," Emma said. "Can I come with you?"

"I was planning to do it online," Zoe said.

Before Emma could convince her sister to take a shopping trip, JJ came back in, followed by a bouncing Calle. She must have run in the second the car came to a complete stop, probably before Dan and Kendra had even unbuckled. The little girl eyed the tree and the presents under it with bulging eyes, explaining her need to be inside so quickly.

"Are any of those for me?" she asked as she pulled her coat off.

"That's rude, Calle," Kendra said as she walked in the door.

"No, it's not," Calle said, hands on her hips. "I just wanted to look."

Emma laughed and looked up as Patrick came back into the room, catching his niece as she launched herself at him. "Hey, squirt," he said. "There might just be a present under there for you, but we have a lot of shopping to do now that I'm back in town."

The doorbell rang again, and Patrick's parents came in with Jake, Shea and Charlie. Ben and Stella Burrows were beaming with happiness, with baby Isobel on her grandfather's hip. Jake helped his wife out of her jacket and helped her settle into a chair before greeting everyone else.

"He treats me like an invalid," Shea stage whispered to Kendra and Zoe, who were sitting across from her. "I'm perfectly healthy and having a normal pregnancy."

"Is that what I have to look forward to?" Zoe asked, casting a look in her husband's direction.

"Absolutely," JJ called over. "I'll be carrying you from room to room soon."

"I'm a little ahead of you," Shea said. "If I can still manage to get around, you'll be fine. Especially with your first."

"We probably should have timed it out better," Kendra said.

"What?" Zoe looked between her business partner and the other women with a look of confusion on her face.

"I'm expecting our third," Kendra said. "But I'm a month or so behind you, so we'll make it work. Luckily, we have good management in place at the restaurant and Palace Plates. Hiring Ann to run the store was genius, and perfect timing since we may overlap in our leave."

"Congratulations," Zoe said, leaning over to hug Kendra. "I can't believe you didn't tell me the other night. How are you feeling?"

Emma half-listened as the women started comparing pregnancy stories, looking over to where Patrick was talking to his father. He met her eyes across the room and winked, gesturing with his head for her to meet him by the Christmas tree.

"Can I have everyone's attention for one minute?" Patrick called out to the room, which quieted quickly.

"Only one?" Jake yelled from the kitchen. "That's not like you."

"Hysterical," Patrick said with an eye roll. "Come in here, please."

Once Jake was perched on the arm of the couch next to where his wife sat, and everyone else was looking at them expectantly, Patrick grinned. "I asked this amazing woman to be my wife, and she foolishly agreed. We're getting married!"

The room erupted as Emma held up her left hand, and everyone rushed at her. Zoe was crying and grabbed her first, hugging her tight. "I'm so happy for you," she whispered in her ear.

Stella was next, admiring the ring and then hugging her tightly. "You're perfect for my boy," she said, bringing tears to Emma's eyes.

Kendra and Shea hugged her and Patrick, complimenting the ring, before the men came forward. JJ hugged her first, kissing her soundly on the cheek before shaking Patrick's hand. "We'll finally be brothers," JJ said. "Welcome to the family."

"As small as we are," Emma said with a laugh, smiling at her sister.

"Welcome to our family," Jake said, kissing her on the cheek. "Are you sure about this guy?"

"Very," she said confidently, smiling back at him.

"Congratulations," Dan said. "We all love you already, and will be happy to officially have you as a Burrows."

"I can't believe it," Emma said. "I just realized I'll be Emma Burrows soon."

"You will," Ben said, pulling her into a bear hug. "I get another daughter, the last and final fit to our family."

"Not counting the babies," Shea called out.

"You're right," Ben said. "Last piece of the next generation."

Emma snuggled in close to Patrick, smiling out at her new family. They had embraced her when she arrived in town with nothing and helped her come out of her shell. Comfortable within their ranks, she had settled into this tiny town and fallen in love with the best man she had ever met. Life was pretty perfect and tonight proved that.

Chapter 9

Patrick sat at the head of the table as they all settled in for dinner. Zoe had directed the reheating process from the stool at the island that JJ had regulated her to, and everything had come out perfect. As usual, she had brought enough food for a small army, but with his nephew Charlie growing more every day, it might all disappear. The two babies were sound asleep in cribs that Patrick had purchased for their use, knowing the family liked to gather at his house each week. Even just when his brothers came to watch a football game, they could bring the kids and have everything they needed.

"Have you started thinking about wedding plans?" Kendra asked the question as she carefully passed a full plate to Calle.

"We have," Patrick responded. "We talked about it earlier, and I have Sean working on some ideas."

"What are you thinking?" Stella asked.

"My first idea was shot down by my thoughtful bride-to-be," Patrick said, squeezing Emma's hand. "An island near Fiji."

"That sounds amazing," Shea said with a sigh.

"I know," Emma responded. "But for you and Zoe to fly that far right now would be a lot. Not to mention the kids. And it's Christmas. We would like to find a way to do it and keep the season in mind. It's my favorite time of year."

Patrick smiled at her, seeing her cheeks turn pink as everyone's eyes were on her when she was talking. "It was very thoughtful of you to think of everyone else," he said. "Sean has a few other options that might play out. We'll give it a couple of days."

"But you're thinking of doing it soon?" Zoe asked, looking surprised. "Like in the next month? I thought the planning alone would take forever."

"Why?" Emma said with a shrug. "I don't need anything special. I just want to marry him. I think you and JJ had the right idea, just do it."

"I could get ordained right now," Dan offered.

"I want to be the officiant if they're doing it that way," Charlie said. "Think of how cool that would be, to say I was the one to marry my uncle."

"The girls would go crazy," Jake said with an eye roll. "I thought you had a girlfriend?"

"Dad," Charlie cried. "Knock it off."

"Oh, okay," Jake said, putting his hands up. "I didn't realize we weren't talking about it. It's not like people don't notice her wearing your jersey at hockey games, or the two of you spending lots of time together."

"You're the worst," Charlie said, his face red. "Can someone make him stop?"

"I don't know how we got off the topic of me," Patrick said, his tone light. "That's unusual."

Charlie shot him a grateful look from the other end of the table as Jake laughed, and everyone started talking at once about the wedding. Emma leaned closer to him, so only he could hear her. "What did Sean say?"

"He's going to make some calls," Patrick said in a low voice. "He had a few local resorts in addition to going out of state. Thought that might be easy and still keep the Christmas spirit. And then he suggested we enjoy the island for our honeymoon if we get a break in filming, which I thought was a great idea."

"Just you and me on a whole island?"

"You okay with that?"

"More than," she said, smiling at him. "I'm just shocked that you don't think Nat and Mike, and Liam and Holly, will somehow find their way to the same place."

"I think for our honeymoon, they'll respect our space," he said. "Unless we want to make it a party. I don't care either way."

"You, me, and a few books sounds perfect," she said. "We wouldn't be able to stay long, if you're in the middle of filming. But a few days would be amazing."

"I don't think I'll be letting you get a lot of reading done," Patrick said with a wink.

Emma laughed. "We'll see how close you are with the script by then, I guess. If you're still studying that, it will give me at least a little time."

"Uncle Patty, I want to go to the beach with you," Calle called out. "Can I come?"

"Not this time, kiddo," he replied. "But we can make plans to go over the summer, okay? When you and Charlie aren't in school, and the new babies are here."

"What are the other options?" Ben asked. "You mentioned Sean had a few ideas."

"We're going to see about doing it at Disney World. Emma deserves to feel like a princess on her wedding day, and where else could make that happen? Plus, they do the holidays there, so it's all decorated," Patrick replied. Seeing Calle's face light up, he held up a hand to caution her. "Before you get too excited, it might not happen. The timing is pretty tight, and it might not work. They were going to see if there was a night they could close early for us, or that we could do it early in the morning, but it's not likely. These things need to be planned out with more notice. But Sean did promise that he would at least plan it for us soon, to stay in the castle and visit the parks."

"Stay inside the castle?" Calle asked, her eyes wide. "All of us?"

"Not all of us," Patrick said with a laugh. "But everyone can visit it. I was thinking you could stay in there with Emma and I, and we would get suites at a resort for everyone else."

Calle nodded quickly. "Yes, I can do that."

"Glad to hear it," he said, smiling at her. "But it's more likely that the wedding will be around here. There are a few mountain resorts that would love to host it, and several hotels in New York and in the Boston area that are also agreeable. It just comes down to what Emma wants."

"I'll look at everything tomorrow," she promised the group.

"In the meantime, we should talk about Christmas," Stella said, artfully changing the subject. "This is becoming a big crowd to shop for. Do we want to do a secret Santa exchange instead of individual gifts?"

"Not including the kids, right?" Jake asked.

"No, just the adults," Ben said. "Kids get gifts from everyone."

"And this doesn't include your own spouse," Stella added. "But it will cut down on having to get gifts for everyone. Zoe and JJ, you wouldn't be getting gifts for almost everyone here, so you're off the hook."

JJ laughed as he nodded. "Thanks. As much as I was looking forward to getting Dan a new tie, I have enough siblings of my own to buy for."

Everyone else agreed to the idea, and Patrick went to grab paper from his office for Stella to make the slips. Once they were all written, they placed them into a Santa hat and passed it around the table.

"Keep it to yourself," Stella called out as Dan pulled the first name.

After a lot of laughs and redraws after people picked their partner, they all had their slips of paper tucked away. Patrick had pulled Shea, and knew he couldn't possibly keep it a secret from Emma. The two women had a close bond, and she would have a better idea of what to get for his sister-in-law than he would. When he tried to peek at the name on her paper, she had laughed and tucked it into her pocket, so finding out hers might be harder.

"Now that we're done, can we watch some football?" Jake asked, pushing back on the table. His service dog quickly appeared from where he had been lying at Jake's feet, ready to move to a new location.

"We should all clean up our plates," Stella called out, bringing Jake back to the table. "We're not leaving Emma with this mess to clean up."

His father and brothers made quick work of cleaning their plate and loading the dishwasher before disappearing to the screening room in the basement, where they could watch the football game on an even larger screen than what was over the fireplace in the living room. Emma was talking to her sister in the kitchen when Patrick brought his plate in and shooed him toward the door to follow his brothers down the stairs. Patrick chose an open recliner next to Jake, with Dan, JJ and Ben on his other side. Jake's service dog Rex was lying on the ground and ignored him as he walked by to sit.

"How are you doing?" Patrick asked Jake after he sat. The other three were having an animated conversation about the game on the television, but Jake seemed more withdrawn.

"I'm good," Jake said. "Sorry, it's been a long week."

"Don't be sorry," Patrick replied. "Anything I can help with?"

"I'm just worried about Shea."

"Shea? Why?" Patrick watched as Rex stood to put his head on Jake's leg, a signal that he was experiencing stress.

Jake's hand started stroking the dog, and Patrick could see some of the anxiety leaving his brother's shoulders.

"Pregnancy is rough," Jake said. "And I already lost one wife. I don't know why, but when she's pregnant, it makes it all so much more to worry about. Will the baby be healthy? Is she doing too much?"

"What does the doctor say?"

"That she's healthy, and the baby is doing great," Jake said. "I'll just feel better when the baby is born and everyone is good."

"And I'm sure that will happen," Patrick assured his brother. "She had one healthy pregnancy, and Isobel is perfect. There's no reason to worry about something different happening this time. But if you're worried, you and Charlie do more around the house. You get up with Izzie and let Shea sleep, or have Charlie do the laundry so Shea isn't doing all that lifting."

"You're right," Jake said with a sigh. "There's just so little time and so much to do."

"I could–"

Jake cut him off with a look. "You don't need to solve this."

"I was just going to offer to get you some help at the house, or with Izzie," Patrick said. "I have Mary in California, and she makes everything work so I don't have to think about a thing. We could get you someone like that."

"I'm not a millionaire," Jake said. "And I'm not letting you pay for that."

"What good is the money if it's just sitting there? I like to help people," Patrick said.

"There are plenty of charities out there that need your support, especially at this time of year. Help them. We're fine." Jake softened his tone after meeting Patrick's eyes. "But I love you for offering."

"Wow," Patrick said, grinning. "This is a big moment. A Christmas miracle, even."

"Knock it off," Jake said, his voice gruffer than usual. "I can still kick your butt if needed."

"Oh, there is never any doubt about that. But I'm going to savor this for a while."

"Savor the feeling of being engaged?" JJ asked from Patrick's other side. "I'm a little jealous. My engagement was too quick to savor."

"That's on you," Patrick said. "What was it? Two hours total? I don't even know if that counts."

"I get things done," JJ said.

"Speaking of, you thew me for a loop on Thanksgiving, when you started asking questions," Patrick said. "I've been meaning to yell at you about that."

"You mean I can't take credit for putting the idea in your head?" JJ asked.

"No," Patrick said. "I knew I was going to do it, and you bringing it up made me so nervous. Emma was convinced I didn't want to marry her, when I was obsessed with keeping my mouth shut to avoid ruining the secret. Couldn't you have waited a few more days before putting your two cents in?"

"I have impeccable timing," JJ said. "But I didn't have any idea it would make things weird. I thought you were on the same page about it."

"We were, but then I got freaked out worrying that she would think I was only proposing because you told me to," Patrick said.

"I kind of like the idea that you'll do what I tell you to, especially since we're going to be brothers. You're stuck with me forever, just like these guys."

"I'd say you could have him, but he's the nicest," Jake said. "Can I give you Dan instead?"

"Boys," Ben said, his voice cutting through the immediate retorts that were ready to fly back and forth. "Let's all play nice for the holidays."

"Does that mean we can say who we got in the draw? Because I'm struggling," Dan said.

"No," Ben said sharply. "Stella is very excited about the secrecy part. Keep it to yourself."

"We can tell our wives, though, right?" Jake asked.

"No one," Ben said.

Jake sighed and sat back in his chair, picking up his beer. Rex laid back at his feet, so the moment of stress had passed. Patrick turned his attention back to the screen as well, but within a minute, his phone started ringing. Everyone yelled at him as he pulled it from his pocket, so he left the screening room and crossed to the gym on the other side of the wall when he saw Missy's name on the screen.

"Hey, Missy," he said as he answered. "What's up?"

"I don't know how, but the news is already out," she said. "Someone spilled about you buying an engagement ring. I'm afraid you're going to be seeing an onslaught of reporters coming to town."

"Now? I was hoping we could get through our local Christmas Festival and Snow Ball before anything spread," Patrick said. "We just told our families. How could it have possibly spread already?"

"That's what I'm trying to find out," she replied. "Let Dan know that I'll be in touch if someone violated their non-disclosure agreement. The jeweler signed one, right?"

"Yes, Sean took care of it before he even told him where he was going," Patrick said.

"Alright, I'll call Sean and see who else might have known," she said. "If you think of anyone, let me know."

"Are they going after Emma again?"

Missy paused, so Patrick knew the news was bad. "Let's just say they are not feeling the spirit of the season. Try to keep her offline as much as you can."

Patrick hung up and resisted the urge to punch the bag that was used for his workouts. Why couldn't people see how amazing Emma was? Or at least just leave her alone. All he wanted was for her to have a perfect holiday season, and this was sure to cause problems. As soon as the press arrived in Vermont, the constant scrutiny would start, which would ruin the season for her. Thinking quickly, he pulled his phone back out and hit the button to call Sean.

"Hey, boss," Sean said as he answered.

"Hey," Patrick said. "Sorry to bother you on a Sunday, but I need you to do something quickly if you can."

"Name it."

"Can you call and book all the rooms at the Inn? And any available Airbnb that you can see in town?"

"Wow, no room at the Inn," Sean said, his voice light. "Who are we subjecting to the true meaning of Christmas?"

"Reporters," Patrick said. "I don't want them here. Let the manager of the Inn know why I'm doing it, and tell him he can rebook the rooms if he's verified that they are not reporters."

"I'll offer to help with that," Sean said. "I know the usual suspects. I'll take care of it."

"Thanks."

"One last thing," Sean said. "Should I be officially offering congratulations, or have you not proposed yet?"

"I did it this morning," Patrick said. "And Emma graciously accepted."

"Congratulations," Sean said. "You two are my couple goals, so I'm really happy for you."

"Thanks," Patrick said. "Now if I can just keep the paparazzi from ruining it for her."

"Let me work my magic, and we'll see what we can do," Sean promised before hanging up.

Patrick went back to join the others watching the game, pretending to focus while mentally reviewing ways to keep Emma in the dark about this. If he could keep the reporters and photographers out of Windsor Peak and keep her off the gossip sites and social media, that would allow her to enjoy the season and not know what was happening. It sounded like he was the one who needed a Christmas miracle to pull this off, but he was willing to try.

Chapter 10

"I feel like people are staring at me," Emma said to her friend Piper as they walked down Main Street. They had met to do some shopping and have lunch, and Emma had felt eyes on her everywhere she went. Piper had been ecstatic when Emma called her with news of the engagement and had wanted to celebrate. The two women had grown close when Emma first moved to town and worked at the bakery for Piper, and had remained friends even after Emma decided to leave the job to focus on the animal rescue.

"Well, you're gorgeous," Piper said. "And the tourists know you're Patrick's girlfriend. Of course they'll stare."

"I wasn't thinking about the crowds who come early before the Festival when we made plans," Emma said. "I feel like there are already a ton of people here. Thursday is when they really start to arrive, isn't it?"

"For the skiers, absolutely," Piper said. "They can get two days in on the slopes before taking part in the weekend activities. But we'll see even more people arrive tomorrow. Is Patrick in hiding?"

"No, we'll be at the Festival on Saturday," Emma said. "He always volunteers to sit at the table with the animal shelter to bring them more attention. We have so many dogs and cats that need to find homes for the holidays, so we're hoping to make that happen."

"I thought you had a ton of them adopted at the Harvest Festival?"

"We did," Emma said. She pulled open the door to the local women's clothing boutique, Finally Dressed, and waved for Piper to go in first. "But the shelter works with others around the country. When they had open spots, they were immediately filled by pulling animals out of kill shelters. If we can find these dogs and cats homes, we can save even more."

"You're amazing," Piper said. "All the work you do with them, and the horse rescue."

"I'm anything but," Emma said with a laugh. "You run a business. Patrick makes movies. Shea is a teacher, Kendra a business owner. I'm just a volunteer."

Piper grabbed her by the arm, making her stop walking. "You are amazing," she said again. "Let yourself believe that."

"Thanks," Emma said softly. "Now, what are we looking for here?"

"I need a dress for the Snow Ball," Piper said. "I know it's last minute, but that's how I work."

"Oh, this will be fun," Emma said. "I do have a closet full if you don't find something, but trying them on is the best part."

She started rifling through the dresses on the racks, pulling out ones that would work with Piper's coloring and the theme. Once she had several options, she pulled Piper to the dressing room and hung them up.

"I can't wear red," Piper said immediately as Emma hung the dress on the wall.

"Why not?"

"It's too showy," Piper said. "I like to blend in. Not to be the center of attention."

"You deserve to be, though," Emma said. "Just humor me and try it on."

Emma settled onto the small couch available for shoppers, waiting for her friend. The bell over the front door chimed as it opened, letting in a gust of cold wind and a small girl. She could possibly be a teenager, if Emma had to guess, but slight. Her clothes didn't fit her right, the pants being an inch too short even on her small frame, and the sweatshirt she wore was way too big. A wool hat that had seen better days was pulled over riotous curls, and she carried a small backpack. She glanced around the shop nervously before spotting Emma on the couch and stepping forward.

"Hi," she said softly. "Is it okay if I sit with you?"

"Sure," Emma said easily. "Are you okay? Is your mom shopping?"

"My mom?" The girl looked comically confused, her brows pulled together as she stared at Emma. "No."

"Okay," Emma said slowly. Her attention was pulled back to the dressing room as Piper emerged, wearing a dress in sage green that looked beautiful, but too big. "Piper, that would be amazing if you had time for alterations. Next year, maybe. Try the red one."

"Are you shopping for a wedding?" The girl asked after Piper disappeared again.

"No, there is an annual charity ball here in town," Emma answered. "We're finding my friend a dress for that."

"Oh." The girl started fiddling with the zippers on her backpack, pulling them back and forth rapidly as she stared at Emma. "But you're getting married, right?"

"Why would you say that?" Emma asked, glancing around the room. It was empty, other than the two of them, and the clerk, who was busy with another shopper.

"You have a big ring," the girl replied, pointing at Emma's left hand.

"Oh," Emma said, feeling relieved. The attention lately made her feel so paranoid, she even suspected this child to be a part of it. "Yes, I am. Or we are. Not this weekend, though."

"When?"

"I'm not sure," Emma said, turning her attention back to Piper as she emerged again. This time, she was wearing a sparkly silver dress that would be stunning if it hadn't washed out her complexion. Piper shook her head as Emma laughed and pointed at the dressing room. "Next."

"Why aren't you sure?" The girl asked, bringing Emma's attention back to her.

Emma considered her words before answering. "We just want some time to enjoy this, and then we'll make some decisions."

"Is it true that you were a foster kid once?"

The sudden shift in topic had Emma struggling to find an answer, so she just nodded. After a moment, she turned to the girl. "What's your name? Are you in the foster system?"

The girl shrugged and stuck her hand into her backpack. Emma's attention was pulled back to Piper as she emerged, and until she saw the look on her friend's face, she didn't know what was happening. But when she turned back, the girl was taking pictures with a cell phone as she backed away from Emma.

"Wait," Emma cried. "What are you doing? Don't do that."

Piper tried to rush forward to grab the phone, but the girl slipped away and out the door before she could grab her. "What just happened? Should we call JJ?"

"No," Emma said with a sigh. "I bet it was a dare. Her friends probably told her to do that."

"Are you sure? That was weird," Piper said. "What was she saying to you?"

Emma ran through their conversation in her head quickly before frowning. "She was asking me if I was getting married, and about the ring. But then she asked about me being a foster kid," she said. "She didn't answer when I asked if she was one, but I think she must be."

"I think we should call JJ," Piper said.

"I'll talk to Patrick about it," Emma promised. "He can help me decide. We won't find her right now anyway, so it's fine. Now, go put on the red dress and stop with the nonsense."

"Did you purposely find dresses that were too big or would look terrible to make me wear the red one?" Piper called out a moment later from behind the door, making Emma stifle a laugh.

When the door opened again, Emma gasped. The red dress fit Piper perfectly, hugging her curves in all the right spots. The neckline plunged just enough to show off her assets without being too revealing, and the skirt was cut to be higher in the front than the back, showing off her shapely legs.

"It's perfect," Emma declared. "We can find you some killer heels and maybe put a piece of holly in your hair. But you should wear your hair down. No one ever gets to see you with it that way."

"No one wants a piece of my hair in their cookie," Piper said with a laugh. "I feel like this is too much. A little black dress would be better."

"No, that would be hiding. This is going to make you the center of attention, which you deserve," Emma said. "You have been so off lately, and I know you've been feeling down. I wish you would tell me what's going on, but that's another discussion. I want you to feel pretty and special for this one night, so you can relax and have fun."

Piper sighed and studied herself for a moment longer in the mirror. "I don't know if you're the best friend I've ever had or the worst," she said with a laugh. "Because I do love this, but I am going to be so nervous."

"Your dance card will be full," Emma said, grinning at her. "I can't wait to see men falling over themselves to get near you."

Piper got a curious look on her face before vanishing into the dressing room, emerging again in her own clothes, carrying the red dress. Emma waited while her friend made the purchase and made arrangements to pick the dress up later, when they were done walking around the downtown area. Once she was done, they pulled on their coats and headed back out, walking toward the Palace for lunch. The restaurant looked busy, but when they entered, Kendra pointed to a small table by the fire, mostly hidden in the corner, for them to take.

Once they settled into their seats and ordered drinks, Emma leaned across the table. "Now you have to tell me your big secret," she said.

"What big secret?"

"You're trying to be coy, but I know something is off with you. It has been for a while," Emma said. "I can't put my finger on it. You can be having a great time with us, and then leave abruptly. It's happened the last few times we have come here for karaoke. Or when we met for drinks last week."

"You're imagining things," Piper said, taking a long sip of her cider. "I get up early, sometimes I just get tired."

"I feel like you're avoiding someone," Emma said. "Is it a man?"

"I just get tired," Piper repeated, a stubborn look in her eye.

"You know you can talk to me about anything, right?"

Piper nodded but avoided Emma's eyes. "I will. Eventually. Right now, just know it has nothing to do with you, okay?"

"Just promise me you won't do it at the Ball," Emma said. "That dress deserves a full night out. Promise."

Piper laughed and nodded. "As if I could say no to you, the sweetest person alive. I'll take a nap on Saturday, I promise."

"Good," Emma said, sitting back in her chair with satisfaction. "I know the Festival will be tiring, but make sure you go home early and get some rest before the Ball starts. We're going to have fun."

***

Patrick was sitting at the kitchen island when she came in from the garage, looking at his phone with a concerned look on his face. When he saw her, he put the phone down and smiled, but she could see tension around his eyes.

"What's wrong?"

"Nothing," he said quickly. "Do you have stuff in the car I can get for you?"

"It can wait," she said. "Tell me what's wrong."

He sighed and ran a hand through his hair. "I wish you couldn't read me so well," he said. "I just got a text from Missy. Apparently, there is a picture of you wearing the engagement ring. People are going crazy on social media. Someone posted it a few hours ago."

Emma felt a pit grow in her stomach. "Let me see."

"No," he said, his tone firm. "You don't need to. You know how people act on there."

"I know, but I just need to see the picture. I won't read the comments, I promise. You can even hold the phone, just show me," she said.

He picked up the phone again and held it out to her, and just as she suspected, the picture was her on the couch at the dress shop. Her left hand was on her leg, the large diamond glowing in the overhead light. Her face was caught in profile, so at least it wasn't her mouth open as she realized what was happening.

"It was a kid," she said. "Maybe twelve or thirteen if I had to guess. She came into the store where Piper and I were shopping and started talking to me. Next thing I knew, she was snapping the picture and running away."

"That's weird," Patrick said. "I figured a reporter snuck into town."

"What do you mean? Had it already gotten out?"

He nodded. "Missy told me on Sunday, but I didn't want to ruin this for you. We had no idea how at the time, but word was out almost immediately. I'm glad I got time to propose before the news broke, at least."

"And tell our families," she said. "That is weird. You've never had issues before with leaks."

"I know," Patrick said. "Sean and Missy did some digging and found out the leak came from the insurance company. The jeweler suggested I insure it before I got on a plane, and I foolishly agreed. Missy and Dan are dealing with the insurance company now, not that it does any good once the news is out. I should have warned you."

"You couldn't have known this would happen," Emma said.

"I know, but I could have made you aware, so you wouldn't be ambushed," he said. "But I did try to keep the reporters from coming to town by booking all the rooms at the Inn."

She laughed and shook her head. "You're incredible," she said, kissing him. "I love you for trying, but I'm not delicate. They won't break me."

"You were so stressed before I went to California, and I thought it was because of all the press," he said. "Then when I was there, I felt like I was a million miles away from you. When you add in the rumors that they were running with, I felt terrible. I hate that this is happening, that it puts a cloud over a happy time for us."

"Nothing could ruin this for me," she told him. "This is the happiest I've ever been, and I don't care what they say. I'm sorry that I seemed distant, I just had a lot on my mind. And I missed you terribly."

"I missed you too," he said. "I hope you know how much you mean to me.

"You've always made me feel loved," she assured him. "I didn't think it was possible to feel this way, until I met you. It was just bad communication on both of our parts. We need to ignore the comments and the press, and just focus on each other. Deal?"

"Deal," he said, pulling her close. "Can we kiss on it instead of shaking?"

Chapter 11

The town's annual Christmas Festival was full of vendors selling everything possible, including handmade ornaments, maple syrup, handmade blankets and sweaters to give as gifts. In addition, several local charities were set up with tables and games to raise funds. The weekend was a huge draw for tourists, who came and spent money in the Festival tent and around town all weekend. The Snow Ball would be held that night in the ballroom of the local Inn to conclude the day.

Patrick spent the morning sitting at the local animal rescue's Christmas Festival table. He had worn a Santa hat, signed autographs, taken countless pictures, and declined to answer the millions of questions regarding whether he was engaged or not. Each time someone asked, he pointed to a puppy in the open pen next to him, asking if they had a chance to meet a dog to consider for adoption. When he finally finished, JJ met him to help him through the crowd to his car. Liam, equally as famous, had taken Patrick's seat at the table and was doing his best to distract everyone from Patrick's departure.

"Things go okay?" JJ asked as they walked.

"Great," Patrick said. "We got a lot of applications, and a few people who want to volunteer. Hopefully, the shelter will be empty by Christmas."

"Only to fill up again," JJ said. "But you do good work."

"Thanks," Patrick said. The crowd thinned once they were outside the tent, and they were able to walk without being stopped by fans. They were halfway to his car, which was parked behind the local church, when a kid ran at him from the opposite side than where JJ was, nearly making him fall. JJ made a move to step between them, but Patrick stopped him. Instead, JJ positioned himself between the kid and Patrick, watching her with a wary look on his face.

"Hi," the girl said. "Umm. I was hoping to talk to you."

"Really?" Patrick said, glancing over at JJ, who looked as confused as him. "What's your name?"

"Eve," she said. "I was just wondering if you're really getting married?"

"Hi, Eve," he said. "It's nice to meet you. Did you happen to meet Emma recently? At a store in town?"

She froze, staring at him as her face paled, before turning back in the direction she had come from. Before she could take off running, JJ had grabbed her by the arm, holding her in place. "Please don't make me run," he said. "You haven't done anything wrong, at least that we know of."

"I haven't," Eve said, her lower lip quivering. "I swear. Someone offered me money to take a picture, and to ask some questions. I just needed it really bad."

"Why?" Patrick asked, keeping his voice low and easy. He didn't want to scare her more than she already was.

"I think they wanted to be able to prove you were engaged," she said. "But then people started saying the ring was fake. I thought if I could talk to you, I could get the money."

"But why do you need the money?"

Eve kicked at the snow with a sneakered toe. "I'm trying to get somewhere."

"Where?" JJ asked. "Did you run away from home?"

"No," she said quickly. "At least, not really. I mean, it's not my home."

"I think maybe we should head to my office and talk," JJ said. He nodded at Patrick and started to walk away with the young girl, still holding her by the elbow . Patrick watched as Eve stomped on JJ's foot and ran off, darting into the crowd leaving the Festival tent and disappearing down the street. JJ was hopping on one foot, scowling at her back.

"Did you just get beaten up by a ten-year-old?" Patrick asked, laughing at his friend.

"This never happened," JJ said.

"Oh, there is no way I can keep this to myself," Patrick replied, still laughing.

"We're supposed to be brothers now," JJ said. "That should offer some secret keeping."

"Do you think I would keep this to myself if it happened to Dan?"

"No," JJ admitted. "Jake, probably."

"Well, he is the scariest. Would you keep it a secret if it happened to Colin or Des?" Patrick asked, referring to JJ's brothers.

"Fine," JJ said, huffing out a breath. "Tell everyone. Embarrass my poor pregnant wife."

"She'll laugh the hardest," Patrick called out as he climbed into his car. He was still laughing as he drove away, beeping at JJ as he limped down the street.

***

Emma had asked him to shower and get ready in his basement spa so that she could have the master bathroom to prep for the evening. They both knew that a lot of pictures would be taken at the Snow Ball, and he knew she was nervous about looking exactly right. He had the easy task of slipping into a tuxedo, which he was so used to wearing, it was like putting on sweatpants. He got as far as the pants, button-down shirt and tie, leaving the jacket on the hanger to pull on just before they left the house.

He went to the kitchen and opened a bottle of wine, pouring two glasses and leaving them on the counter before sitting down. A quick scroll through his phone showed him that speculation about his upcoming nuptials had reached a fever pitch. Missy had texted earlier, encouraging him to answer questions honestly and allow Emma to show off the ring. She had offered to fly in from New York, but he had told her to stay put, figuring they could handle it. The Ball would primarily be for Windsor Peak locals, and he had his family there to help if need be.

116

The sound of Emma coming down the stairs had him standing and turning in that direction. When she came around the corner, she took his breath away. The ice-blue dress shimmered in the Christmas lights, and a long slit up the front revealed her right leg as she walked. The dress was sleeveless, and her hair was pinned up on her head.

"You look stunning," he said, moving toward her.

She blushed and glanced down at herself. "Are you sure? I feel like this might be wrong. I have a green dress too, maybe I should change?"

"You look beautiful. You literally took my breath away."

"You're either incredibly sweet or a great liar," she said.

"Can I kiss you, or would I ruin your makeup?" he asked, taking her into his arms.

She laughed and leaned in. "I haven't put my lipstick on yet."

"You're a genius," he said. After kissing her thoroughly, he moved to hand her a glass of wine. "Smart and beautiful. How did I get so lucky?"

"I'm the lucky one," she said. "Look at what you have done for my life. Took me from an ordinary person to all of this."

"You were never ordinary," he said.

"Patrick," she said, rolling her eyes. "I was broke, and no one even knew I existed. Now I have people sneaking pictures of me anytime I go anywhere. I'd say I went from ordinary to extraordinary due to you."

"Speaking of," he said. "I can't believe I forgot to tell you. JJ and I met the girl who took the picture of the ring as we were leaving the Festival."

"Really? How do you know it was her?"

"She told me," he said. "Right after she came running up to us and asked me if we were engaged. When I asked about the picture that was taken of you, she spilled everything. Said she was offered money to get a picture of the ring, and to confirm our engagement."

"And she obviously needs it," Emma said, with a worried look on her face. "She looked young to be that desperate. I know that feeling."

"I know you do," he said. "We'll try to find her, make sure everything is okay. But that will be tomorrow. Tonight, we are going to dance and be merry."

"She asked me if I was a foster kid," Emma said as Patrick helped her with her coat. "Maybe JJ could see if someone from the system is missing? I have a feeling she ran away."

"Me too," he said, pulling on his tuxedo jacket before pulling a long, black wool coat out of the closet to wear over the suit. "I asked as much. She gave a confusing answer. I'll talk to JJ about it first thing tomorrow. Tonight, can we focus on us? And on the Christmas spirit? I want to make sure you enjoy this."

"A night of dancing to Christmas music in your arms? I can promise I'll enjoy it," she said, walking towards the door to the garage.

***

Patrick parked in the small lot behind the Windsor Palace, where they were meeting his family and their friends for a drink before walking to the Inn together. The restaurant was nearly empty, with most of the locals at home preparing for the Snow Ball, so they had the bar to themselves. Kendra had offered to close entirely so her staff could attend the festivities, but a few of the college students home on break had offered to work so they could serve the few tourists not attending. She was behind the bar herself, passing out glasses of wine and whiskey to her family when Patrick and Emma arrived.

After greeting everyone, Emma was pulled into conversation with the other women while Patrick stood with his brothers and the other men. Jake handed him a whiskey before sitting back on his barstool, then turned to face his brother. "Is tonight the big night? Will you two be announcing the engagement officially?"

"No," Patrick said. "We changed our minds on the drive here. We'll tell people we know but ask them to keep it quiet but hold off on a big announcement."

"Why?" Dan asked, frowning. "I thought you had it planned out?"

"We did, but something weird happened today," Patrick told them. "Emma wants to figure that out before we do anything else."

"What happened?" Jake asked, glancing between him and JJ. "Obviously we missed something. You're both acting weird."

"Did you see the picture of Emma with the ring?" When everyone nodded, Patrick continued. "Apparently, it was taken by a young girl when Emma and Piper were out shopping. The kid said something to Emma about being in the foster system, and today she told me that she was hoping to get money if she could confirm we were engaged."

"But if you just announce it tonight, no one will benefit from it financially," Dan said. "I thought the idea was one big reveal since insurance company already dropped the ball about the ring. The plan was for you two to go public tonight and announce the engagement, and your publicist would release an official statement at the same time."

"That was the plan," Patrick said. "But Emma would rather wait. Seeing this little girl, who's probably a runaway from a foster house, has rocked her. If this kid needs help that much, we're worried she'll run off the promise of money disappears. JJ spooked her today before she kicked his butt, so we're trying to be careful."

"What's that now?" Mike asked, leaning over from where he was sitting at the bar. "JJ got beat up by a kid?"

"He did," Patrick said, at the same time JJ said no.

"She stomped on my foot," JJ said. "I wasn't expecting it, that's all."

"Did you put out an alert about the violent criminal?" Liam asked as he laughed. "She could be a danger to anyone. We'll all need to be on high alert."

"Go ahead, make fun," JJ groused. "But if she comes along tonight, I'm telling her to stomp on you. You'd be surprised how much power she has for such a petite person."

"I'm sure she has special forces training," Jake said, laughing.

"Is it time for us to go yet?" JJ asked, looking at his watch dramatically before looking over to where his wife was standing. "Darling, the boys are picking on me. Can we get moving?"

"Sure," Zoe said. "Stay behind me. I'll protect you from any children on the street."

"Hysterical," JJ said, as everyone else laughed.

They all gathered their coats and headed out the front door for the short walk to the Inn. Even though it was less than a block, they were stopped several times along the way, since Patrick, Liam and Natalie were a novelty sight for tourists. Once they arrived at the Inn, the small group of press outside jumped into action, calling for them to stop for pictures alone and with their significant others. Liam's girlfriend, Holly, disappeared into the building with the others, leaving Liam to appear to be attending the Ball solo with the other two famous couples.

"Emma, can we see the ring?" One photographer called out as they snapped pictures, causing the others to join in the fray. Emma, wearing gloves, simply smiled at them as Patrick started to lead her away. "Patrick, just one picture of you both with the ring! Emma!"

The noise ended as soon as they were in the lobby of the Inn, which was clear of any press. A few security guards were visible, and Patrick appreciated that the manager had taken extra steps to keep them out. The lobby was decorated for Christmas, with a giant tree in one corner, and an elaborate gingerbread depiction of downtown Windsor Peak in the opposite corner. A train ran below the Christmas tree, stockings were hung over the fireplace, and decorations seemed to cover every inch. Emma was gazing around in wonder, but took Patrick's arm so he could lead her into the ballroom.

Once inside, she gasped in wonder, making him smile. Shiny snowflakes hung from every inch of the ceiling, and snow appeared to glimmer underfoot thanks to carefully placed lights. The tables were draped in ice blue and silver, with a centerpiece designed to look like snowmen. Christmas trees flocked to look snow covered, draped in ribbon and were decorated with handmade ornaments from the youth center. More white and blue lights were strategically placed around the room, adding to the feeling that they were outside in a winter wonderland. Patrick glanced up, catching a glimpse of the mistletoe above them at the same time Emma did, and kissed her softly after appreciating the smile it had brought to her face. Seeing that childlike wonder on her face brought more joy to his heart than he would have ever thought possible, and he was determined to keep it alive for her through the holiday.

Chapter 12

Emma felt like she was floating as she and Patrick walked into the house just after midnight. They had stayed at the Ball until the lights came on, dancing and enjoying time with their friends and neighbors. The night had been magical, and she wished it could have gone on forever.

"That was the best night," she said to Patrick as she slipped off her high heels. "I wish it hadn't ended so quickly."

"We were there for almost five hours," he said, pulling her close to him. "But I'm up for one more dance if you are."

She nodded, and he called over to their smart speaker to play her favorite Christmas song. The fact that he knew the exact right song to play proved once again that he was her person, and she settled her head on his chest with a sigh. They danced around the kitchen in silence, only the lights from the Christmas tree shining in the room.

"I'm glad you had fun," he said as the song came to an end.

"Because I was with you," she said. "And all our closest people. It really did put me in the holiday spirit, more than I was before. I can't believe we're only two weeks away from Christmas now. I want this time to go slowly so I can savor it."

"Then we're off to Scotland," he said as they walked up the stairs. "But I'll make sure we're back before Zoe has the baby. Or at least that you can be, if I'm still shooting."

"I didn't think of that," she said. "But you're right, I'll want to come back."

"And then there's the matter of our wedding to deal with," he said. "With all that's been going on this week, we really haven't put much thought into it. Sean had a couple of options that could work, if we still want to try and get it done now."

"That sounds so unromantic," she said. "Like we're rushing things, when it's really just that I'm anxious to start our lives together. But I am distracted by the situation with Eve, and I'd feel better if that was taken care of before we think about the wedding."

"I agree," he said. "I think we're better off waiting, as long as you're okay with it."

"I am," she said. "I know it will be hard, but these months will fly by. Of course, all the babies being due around then complicates that timing as well. I hate to think of anyone having to put on a bridesmaid dress after they just had a baby."

"I know," he said. "I've been trying to see if there is a gap in the schedule where we could sneak home for a few days and have a quick wedding. They're being so tight with the script and the plans, I'm afraid we won't know until it's here, and we can't pull off a big wedding with less than twenty-four-hour's notice."

"And having it in Scotland doesn't work well with three pregnant family members," she said. "Not to mention their busy lives. We can't expect everyone to drop everything to meet us somewhere, or for them to pull Charlie and Calle out of school."

"We'll figure it out," he said. "When we're not so tired."

"First priority is finding Eve," Emma reminded him. "I need to know that she's safe and okay. Then we can think about the wedding."

"JJ and I talked about her tonight," he said. "And we'll see what we can do in the morning. I also thought that I could hire a private investigator if we need to."

"Let's see if we can find her first," Emma said. "I don't want to spook her. I just want to make sure she has a roof over her head and people to celebrate Christmas with. It feels unfair that I have all of this now, and there are kids like her out there with potentially nothing."

"And that's why I love you," Patrick said, taking her in his arms again. "Your heart never ceases to amaze me. You have so much to give everyone around you, even strangers."

"And the horses," she said with a laugh. "But it's why I love you back. You're the same way."

"Guess it's a good thing I convinced you to spend your life with me, huh?" he asked before kissing her so thoroughly she could barely remember her own name, never mind what she had been worried about. Better to focus on the man in front of her and the feeling of joy she had found.

***

Emma woke the next morning to the smell of coffee brewing and no sign of Patrick anywhere. She stumbled into the bathroom and took a quick shower to wake herself up before throwing on jeans and a warm sweater. Once she emerged downstairs, she saw that he had already built a fire and started cooking breakfast. He had his back to her, and was wearing only a pair of pajama bottoms featuring dogs dressed as Santa's reindeer, and was singing a Christmas carol as she came into the room. She paused to soak in the scene, reminded once again that she was the luckiest woman on the planet that this man loved her. His pre-movie workouts had him finely sculpted, ready to appear with his eight-pack on the screen. Even from behind, his muscled back was enough to make a grown women drool, and he was hers.

"Good morning," she said, hugging him from behind. He turned, a spatula high in the air, to hug and kiss her properly before turning back to his skillet.

"Morning, my darling," he said. "I'm making us some breakfast burritos so we can have good sustenance before we start our hunt."

"Our hunt?"

"For Eve."

"What?" She stared at him, not following. "Christmas Eve is still two weeks away."

"No, the girl," he said. "Her name is Eve. Did I not tell you that?"

"I don't think you did," she said. "But now I'm with you. What's our plan?"

"I texted JJ already," he said. "He's off today, but he called down to tell his officers to keep an eye out. There is one small shelter that we can check, but otherwise he can't think of anywhere else that a teenage girl would be staying and not bringing attention to herself."

"Maybe a barn?" Emma suggested, a smile on her face.

"Only the most special think to do that," Patrick said, kissing her again. "But not a bad idea to check some of the properties that are more remote and might have outer buildings."

"It would have to be walking distance to town," Emma said. "Unless she has a car. But she didn't look old enough to drive."

"Let's start with the smaller search area," he said. "And go from there. JJ did have a suggestion."

"What was it?"

"That she might come to us," he said. "If we just go out and be seen, she might turn up. It's not a bad idea."

"Okay," Emma said slowly. "Just wander around town?"

"Today is the gingerbread house contest at the library," Patrick said. "And they are doing ice skating in the park at the pond, along with an organized snowball fight this afternoon. They'll have hot chocolate and food trucks set up, so it will draw a crowd."

"That works for me," Emma agreed. "Makes more sense than wandering the town searching. That seems like a needle in a haystack search. If she'll find us, that makes things easier."

"We have a plan for finding her," Patrick said, handing Emma a plate of food. "Now, what do we do once we find her?"

"Find out what her story is," Emma said. "See if she needs help."

"We can't bring her here," Patrick said, his voice kind. "I know you'll want to, and I would too. But we can't set ourselves up to be front page fodder."

"I know," Emma said. "But hopefully she does have a place to stay. Or we can help with that, maybe?"

"Okay, let's just find her and then we can figure it out," Patrick said. "I just wanted to make sure we were on the same page about bringing anyone here."

***

Patrick was stopped every few minutes to take a selfie with a fan or to sign an autograph. One young boy ran up to him, holding an action figure of Patrick's superhero character, which made them both laugh. He had taken a picture with the boy and the toy, and asked Emma to take one for his own social media team to use.

"I feel like we're too out in the open here," Emma said as they strolled down Main Street. "The two times she approached us, we were alone. Or nearly alone."

"You're right," Patrick said, glancing around. "The outdoor seating area at the coffee shop is empty. Why don't we get a hot drink and sit there for a bit?"

"Perfect." They crossed the street, waving to some familiar faces as they made their way to the coffee shop. Once they arrived, she gestured to the empty area in front. "Want to sit and I'll run in?"

"No, you relax," he said. "I'll be right back."

Emma sat facing the street but was distracted by an incoming text message. After replying to Zoe, she looked up and caught sight of the girl they were looking for. She was standing halfway hidden by the town's gigantic Christmas tree in the center of the square, but there was no mistaking it was her. When their eyes met, she started to duck back, but hesitated when Emma waved to her. Emma waved again, beckoning her over to where she sat, and was afraid to take her eyes off the girl to look for Patrick. After a painful moment, the girl stepped fully into view and started walking toward Emma, her head down.

Emma took a quick second to glance inside, seeing Patrick talking to a small crowd of people, and wasn't able to get his attention. When she looked back, the girl was coming up the few steps to the porch, hesitating when she got to the top. Smiling brightly, Emma gestured to the chair next to her.

"Come sit," she said. "Please."

After another brief hesitation, she moved forward. Rather than taking the chair that Emma had pointed at, which would have placed her between Emma and the building, she chose one near the edge of the porch. She didn't want to be trapped in place, Emma realized, her heart hurting for the girl.

"I'm Emma," she said gently. "I understand your name is Eve?"

"Yes," she said, nodding slightly as she looked at her lap.

"Patrick told me that someone offered you money to get a picture of me?"

"Yes," she said again, her voice even softer. "But then they wanted me to do more, and they wouldn't pay me unless I did."

"Do you know who it was?"

"No," Eve said, shaking her head. "It was a guy, but he just gave me the phone and told me what to do. Then I texted him the picture like he said, but he wanted more."

"You asked me about the foster system. Am I right in thinking that's where you are now?"

"I have an aunt," Eve said in a burst of energy. "I don't think she knows about me. But I thought if I could get the money, and get some nice clothes and get to her, maybe she would let me live with her."

"How old are you?" Emma asked.

"Sixteen," Eve said, straightening her shoulders as she spoke. At Emma's look, she sighed. "Twelve."

"And what happened to your parents?"

Eve shrugged, avoiding Emma's eyes. "My mom left when I was a baby. I don't remember her. My dad kept me for a few years, but I guess I cried too much or something. He left one day and just never came back."

"You know it's not your fault, right?" Emma asked, her heart breaking for this little girl who had been dealt a terrible hand in life.

Eve shrugged. "That's what they say. But I hear lots of things from the other kids, and who knows what was wrong with them. All that matters is they didn't want me. But then I was able to get more information about my mom, and the librarian helped me find old yearbooks at her high school. I found out I have an aunt, and I was able to find her on Instagram. And she has to be better than them, right?"

Patrick came out of the coffee shop, causing Eve to tense until he placed three hot cups on the table and a bag filled with pastries before taking his seat. "I got us all some hot chocolate," he said. "And some food. I was hoping you would join us, Eve."

"I was just telling Miss Emma that I'm sorry I caused her problems," Eve said. "And I'm sorry I hurt your friend."

"Oh, I'm not," Patrick said, his voice easy. "It gives me something to make fun of him for. But the next time the police want to talk to you, please do me a favor and don't run. Most aren't as kind as JJ and wouldn't take kindly to that."

"I'll try," Eve promised. She took a sip of the hot chocolate and closed her eyes, smiling slightly as she swallowed. Patrick opened the bag and gestured for her to take a treat, and once she had half a croissant in her mouth, she seemed to relax further.

"Where have you been staying?" Emma asked, hoping not to spook her but needing to know.

Eve paused, the food halfway to her mouth, and stared at Emma with wide eyes. She seemed to be battling with herself as she took another bite and finally sighed before she spoke. "The library."

"Really?" Emma asked, thinking of the building. "I love it there. Being surrounded by all those books is the best. But how are you doing that?"

"I hide until they close," Eve said, staring at the table. "I swear, I'm not doing anything bad. I just had to find a place to sleep inside. It was so cold out. And I can't go back where I was. I just can't."

"It was that bad?" Emma wanted to reach for her hand, knowing some of what she must have been through. But the fear that she would run again and they wouldn't be able to help kept her from doing so.

"Yes," Eve said, a single tear streaking down her cheek. "Please don't tell anyone."

"We won't," Patrick promised. "But we can't have you staying there. You could get into a lot of trouble. We'll figure something out, okay? Just promise us one thing."

"What?" Eve asked, her eyes darting between them. Emma's heart ached at the wariness she saw in them.

"You won't run again," Patrick said. "We're invested now, and we want to make sure you're safe."

"I thought you would want me to swear I won't talk to them about you," Eve said. "The media, I mean."

"I don't care about that," Patrick said. "I care about you being safe. Can you sit with Emma while I make some calls? I'll find a safe place, and then we'll see about getting in touch with your aunt. I want to make sure that this is a good solution before I do anything else."

Eve nodded, and Emma finally gave in to the temptation to reach over and squeeze her hand. They might be many years apart, but they had been through the same losses, and both knew what it felt like to be alone in the world. Emma was lucky that she had found Zoe and met Patrick along the way. If she could pay that forward with Eve, she would do everything she could to find her the same security and safety she had found.

Chapter 13

Patrick crossed the street to the Windsor Palace, which was starting to get crowded with hungry families for lunch. JJ's brother Desmond was wiping down the bar when Patrick came in, and grinned at him. "Hey, man," he said. "Haven't seen you at poker night in a while. Glad you're back in town."

"Thanks," Patrick said. "I'm glad to be back. I'll probably join you guys tomorrow, if things go well today."

"We're wearing ugly sweaters," Des said. "And bringing gag gifts for a swap. Hopefully, your brothers told you."

"They did," Patrick said. "I'm hoping Emma will come along too. It sounds like they'll have their own little party while we play."

"Wouldn't know," Des said with a laugh. "I'm happily single."

"Don't dare the universe like that," Patrick warned him. "Hey, I need to make some calls. You mind if I go back and use Kendra's office?"

"Go for it," Desmond said, waving toward the kitchen door. "If you need anything, let me know."

Patrick ducked into the small office, closing the door behind him. Once he had pulled off his heavy jacket, he unlocked his phone and hit the button to call Dan. After two rings, his brother picked up. "Ho ho ho," he said. "Santa hotline."

"Daddy!" Calle's voice came through the phone followed by her laughter. "You're so silly."

"Oh, I have it backwards," Dan said. "This must be Santa calling me. Give me a minute to talk to him."

"Santa, huh?" Patrick asked, listening as the noise around Dan started to fade.

"It's the only way to get a minute of peace around here," Dan said. "I forget how amped up the kids get as we get closer to the big man's arrival. What's up with you?"

"Emma and I found the girl that we've been looking for," Patrick said. "The one who took the picture of the ring and asked me about the engagement. She's just a kid, and she ran away from her foster home. It sounds like it wasn't a great place, and they probably haven't even reported her missing. I need to find her a safe place to live, and then help her get in touch with an aunt who she found on social media."

"Oh, man," Dan said. "That's a lot. Dealing with the system can be difficult. They aren't going to let you place her somewhere that hasn't been fully vetted. You'd have to find an existing foster family that could take her, and even that could have a lot of red tape. Not to mention the aunt could be a nightmare, you know that, right? Or what if it's not really her aunt?"

"I know, but I have to try something," Patrick said. "Emma and I already agreed that it's not an option to bring her home with us. And I happen to have a brother who's an amazing lawyer and a best friend who is the head of the sheriff's department. If you two can't get this done, no one can."

"I'm glad I don't have to be the one to tell you that you can't take her home with you," Dan said.

"Which means we need to find her a place that's safe," Patrick continued. "Do you still have that private investigator's number? Can you ask him to dig into the aunt?"

"Yes," Dan said. "Send me her name and whatever information the girl has about her."

"Who would I call about a better foster placement for her? Maybe something here in town, so I can keep an eye on her?"

"I can ask about that too, but JJ might be better equipped," Dan said. "Or know who to talk to."

"Alright, I'll call him now. Thanks for your help." Patrick ended the call and quickly called JJ, who answered right away.

"Hey, Patrick," JJ said. "Des was just telling me you're in Kendra's office. I'm at the bar."

"Can you come back here? I need to talk to you about something in private," Patrick said. When JJ agreed, he hung up the phone and checked quickly for any text messages from Emma, worried Eve may have run off again. Seeing none, he tucked the phone into his pocket as JJ came into the room.

"What's up?" JJ asked. "This was good timing. I just popped in to say hi to Des before I grabbed some groceries. You guys want to come over for the game today?"

"I don't know that we'll be able to, but I'll keep you posted," Patrick said. "But first, we found Eve. The girl that beat you up."

"Okay, she didn't," JJ said, shaking his head. "Never mind. You found her, and now what?"

"I need to find her a safe place to stay," Patrick said. "A foster parent here in town, maybe, who we trust."

JJ sat back in his seat and scratched his chin, looking deep in thought before reaching for his phone. "Let me call someone," he said.

Patrick listened to the one-way conversation JJ was having, seeing the frustration on his friend's face. When JJ hung up, he held up one finger to Patrick and then put the phone back to his ear.

"Hey," he said. "Quick question for you. Are you guys still listed as foster parents? Good. How do you feel about possibly taking in one tonight? Yes, like today. Alright, thanks. I'll call you back."

JJ hung up and Patrick leaned forward, anxious to hear the answer. "Well?"

"They'll take her," he said. "I'll call social services and smooth things over. They were trying to tell me that they had to bring her in themselves and go through the proper channels, but that's not acceptable. I know they have a lot going on, but it's ridiculous to make her go back somewhere that she doesn't feel safe. I'm glad I thought of the better option, I should have started there. But this way, we can still go through the right procedure so it will all be legal."

"And you're sure it's a safe place?"

"Beyond positive."

"How can you be so sure?" Patrick asked. As much as he wanted to believe in all his neighbors, Emma would never forgive herself if they put Eve into a dangerous situation.

"Because they raised the best kid on the planet," JJ said. When Patrick looked at him with confusion, JJ laughed. "Me. My parents are registered as foster parents, they just haven't taken anyone in lately. In Boston, they had kids coming and going when they had an empty nest. Now that Colin has been home, they hadn't thought of it. But he's ready to move out, so the timing is perfect."

"Are you sure? I mean, it sounds perfect. But I don't know anything about this girl, and it could end up being a nightmare," JJ said. "Plus, it's almost Christmas. That's a lot for them to take on."

"My parents dealt with four of us," JJ said. "They've got this."

***

Patrick was glad to see Emma and Eve still sitting at the table where he had left them when he finally emerged from Windsor Palace. He crossed the street and reclaimed his seat, noticing as he did that Eve was shivering in the cold. Pulling off his jacket, he stood again to drape it over her shoulders before sitting again.

"Good news," he said. "We have a workable solution. JJ is working on the final details, but we have a safe foster place for Eve to stay while we track down her aunt."

"I can't," Eve said. "Please, don't make me go back to one of them."

Emma looked at Patrick with wide eyes, and he could see the same panic that he heard in Eve's voice. He spoke quickly, wanting to put them both at ease. "It's not what you're used to. I promise. And if you don't like it, we'll find something else. But these are people we know and trust."

"Who is it?" Emma asked.

"JJ's parents," Patrick said. Turning back to Eve, he continued. "You'd be the only other person in the house. JJ's brother had been staying there, but he'll stay with one of his siblings for the next few weeks. He was already due to move out any day now, and said he doesn't mind. It was all discussed with the Monahan family on a very loud group call. Colin was more than happy to stay with Desmond, and their parents are excited to have a new kid in the house."

"They don't even know me," Eve said. "I could be a terrible person."

"You could be," Patrick said, nodding. "Or you could be a good person in a terrible situation. I hope having a good night's sleep in a safe place will help you feel a lot better about your place in life."

"Maggie and Tim are good people," Emma said. "Will you at least meet them?"

Eve nodded slowly, and Patrick stood, not wanting to give her time to reconsider. "Come on, I'll drive us all there."

***

Patrick led the way up to the front door of the Monahan house, glancing over at Eve when they waited for the doorbell to be answered. She looked terrified, and he smiled at her reassuringly. "I promise, if you don't feel good about this, we'll all leave together and figure something else out."

"Can't I just stay with you?" Eve whispered to Emma, who shook her head.

"I'm sorry," Emma said. "We aren't foster parents, and I think it's better for you if you go through the proper channels. This way, if your aunt wants to take you to live with her, she can do it the right way."

Eve sighed, but Patrick noticed she nodded slightly just before the door opened. Maggie Monahan was there, smiling and gesturing for them to walk through the door. "Come in, come in," she said. "This was just the best treat for us. Thank you so much for thinking of Tim and I."

"I can't take credit for that," Patrick said. "JJ jumped right on it. I had no idea you had done some fostering."

"Yes, back when we still lived in Massachusetts," Maggie said. "Here, let me take your coats. Tim is just in the kitchen making some hot chocolate for everyone."

They waited while she hung their coats on the pegs by the door and then led them to the kitchen. It was warm and bright, with clean white countertops and dark cabinets. Tim was stirring something on the stove and smiled at them. "Welcome," he said. "Maggie put some cookies in the oven when JJ called, and I thought cocoa would be perfect with them."

"Here, sit," Maggie said, gesturing to the large table. She bustled around the kitchen for a minute and returned with a tray of steaming cookies and some napkins. Tim followed with mugs to hand out, and soon they were all settled around the table. "Now, let me tell you about us, Eve. My husband and I have been married for a long time, and we raised four kids. Three boys and one girl. I think you've met JJ, but our other three are Colin, Desmond and Finley. They all live locally. Colin had been staying with us, but he was planning to move out on the first of the year. He's going to stay with his brother Desmond while you're with us, so you'll be the only kid at home. The rest of them do come and go, but you'll get to know them, and I think you'll like them."

"The kids are all grownups," Tim said with a laugh. "But the boys rarely do their own laundry. Other than JJ, but he's married, so he had to start doing it himself."

"We decided to become foster parents when our youngest two went to college," Maggie continued. "Over the years, we've had everyone from babies to nearly eighteen-year-olds with us. We keep in touch with almost all of them, but obviously it's a little harder to talk to the youngest. But we get Christmas cards from a lot of them, so I can show you."

"We were wondering something," Tim said. "Since your name is Eve. Were you born on Christmas Eve?"

Eve nodded. "Yes," she said.

"Oh, how exciting," Maggie said, clapping her hands. "We have a double celebration coming up."

Eve nodded and took a cookie from the tray, her eyes widening when she took a bite. "This is delicious."

"My grandma's secret recipe," Maggie told her. "I'll teach you how to make them."

"Really?"

"Absolutely," Maggie said. "Do you want to tell us a little about yourself? Or would you rather see the house?"

Eve hesitated, then took a sip of her hot chocolate and studied the table as she talked. "My mom left when I was a baby. I don't really remember her at all. My dad stayed for a few years and then left me one day. The neighbors heard me crying and called for help. I've been in foster homes since then."

"How many?" Maggie asked gently, reaching over to hold the girl's hand. Patrick was shocked to see Eve accept the gesture and hold tight in return.

"Twenty-three," Eve said. "This will be twenty-four."

"I can promise you one thing," Tim said, clearing his throat. "If you decide to stay here with us, this will be your last. Whether you find a family member to take you, or you stay here until you're ready to be an adult, this is a safe place for you. No one will hurt you. We'll ask you to help with the dishes, and to do your homework, but we won't ever do anything to hurt you."

Eve nodded, and a tear slipped down her cheek. Patrick's heart ached at the sight, thinking of all the girl had probably been through over the years. He reached for Emma's hand, seeing her own emotion as well. She had been down the same path as Eve, although she had started at an older age and found kindness quickly, avoiding some of the horror stories he guessed Eve had survived.

"Would you like to see the house?" Maggie asked. Eve nodded, and they both stood up from the table. "Do you feel safe here? Would it be okay for Patrick and Emma to go?"

Eve glanced at them, chewing her lip as she thought. "Yes, it's okay," she said finally. "Thank you. For this."

"Absolutely," Emma said. "We're still here for you. Don't think this is us dropping you off and forgetting about you. We'll be checking in regularly, and you have my number if you need it."

"I won't give them any more information about whether you're engaged or not," Eve said, ducking her head. "You've been so nice, I couldn't do that."

"We appreciate that," Patrick said. "I think the word is out anyway, but thank you."

"Thank you," Eve said. She walked away with Maggie, glancing over her shoulder once and exchanging a look with Emma that Patrick couldn't read.

"Tim, you have our numbers if anything happens," Patrick said. "Call anytime."

"We will," Tim promised as he walked them to the door. "This is exciting for us. Maggie is over the moon to have a kid in the house again to fuss over. She's been planning out Christmas activities since we got the call. She almost had me convinced to take the tree down so we could decorate with Eve, but we ran out of time."

"We're just so happy she has a safe place to stay," Emma said. "I hope the aunt actually exists and would want her, but I'm even happier to know she's somewhere that I know is safe and happy."

"She'll be both," Tim said. "Stop by anytime to see her."

They said goodbye and walked down the snowy path to Patrick's SUV, which was parked at the curb. He opened the door and helped Emma in before going around to the driver's side. After starting the car, he looked over at her before driving away. "Are you okay?"

Chapter 14

"I haven't thought about those days in a long time," Emma said. "And I was pretty lucky. I had some bad places, but nothing like what I think Eve has been in. I hope she'll be alright."

"Maggie and Tim are good people," Patrick said. He pulled slowly away from the house, heading towards home. "We can call and check in later tonight. But I think she'll find she's so happy there, maybe there isn't a need to find the aunt."

"She still should," Emma said. "It's nice to have some family ties. But if that falls apart, at least she won't be lost again. She has something to keep her safe."

"You made her a Christmas miracle," Patrick said. "You are an angel."

"Stop," Emma said with a laugh.

"No, I'm serious," he said. "Most people would have been furious at the intrusion on their privacy. Or forgotten about it entirely. But you put her wellbeing above anything else, and made sure this happened. Don't discredit what you did."

"Thank you," she said. "For your words, and also for making this happen. You were just as big a part of it as I was."

"But I would have forgotten about her entirely after the story came out," he said. "My instinct is to avoid people who come into my life just for their own benefit. You did the opposite. That's what impresses me so much."

"Enough about me," she said with a laugh. "You know I get embarrassed. Let's talk about the wedding. I know we put it on the back burner while we figured out Eve's situation, and I appreciate your patience about it. But now we need to make some actual decisions."

"You're right," he said. He pulled the car into the garage and waited until they had walked into the house before talking again. "Want me to open a bottle of wine, or is it too early?"

"Let's wait," she said. "I'm still savoring the sugar high."

"Okay, then let's talk wedding." Patrick sat on the couch facing the Christmas tree and patted the cushion next to him. Once she was settled, he pulled her close and leaned back. "We ruled out the island because it's just too far for everyone. Even once the babies are born, it's a long way to travel with infants. Sean has some hotels in New York and Boston that would love to have us, and even a few in California. Plus, he talked to one in Stowe that would be close by and easy. Any of those are willing to fit us in any date that we want."

"I don't know how I feel about a wedding at a hotel," she admitted. "I feel like it just invites attention. Word will get out, and we'll have people sneaking in to get pictures. I don't want to feel like I'm on show when I want to be focused on us."

"That's a good point," he said. "I'll tell Sean to go back to the drawing board. Since we already decided to wait, we have some time to figure it out."

"I'm sorry that this whole thing with Eve took up so much time," Emma said. "I feel bad."

"Don't," he replied. "Something wonderful happened. We're together and committed, and it's okay to wait a few months to make it legal. I'm not going anywhere, and we can enjoy the engagement for a while. It doesn't matter to me if we get married tomorrow or ten years from now. We're in this for the long haul."

"Are you sure?"

"Yes," he said. "The movie is going to take a long time to film. Maybe we'll find time in the middle to have the wedding, and then we can focus on starting a family."

"Right away?" She asked, surprised. They had talked about having a baby many times but hadn't discussed the timing.

"Do you want to wait?"

"No," she said. "I just want to make sure that when it happens, you'll be able to enjoy it. And be here for everything. I don't want you to miss a major moment because you're off doing press or have another commitment."

"After this movie wraps, I have a break before we film again," he said. "And for all I know, they'll kill me off in this one."

"You know they won't," she said with a laugh. "You're the favorite. And your character is immortal."

"I always forget that part," he said with a sigh. "But at some point, I'll be too old, and they'll find a way to get rid of me."

"I won't," Emma said. "You're stuck with me until we're both using walkers and complaining about sore feet."

"Sounds like a deal," he said, leaning down to kiss her. "I couldn't ask for anything more than that."

***

The next few days passed in a blur of shopping, wrapping, and opening Christmas cards. Emma had checked in regularly with Eve and Maggie Monahan, and they were getting along like old friends. Eve was slowly coming out of her shell, and Maggie was excited to bring her to a family dinner over the weekend so she could meet the rest of the family.

Emma had just placed the last present under the tree when she heard Patrick, Mike, Dan and Jake coming up from the gym. They had been working out for almost two hours, their loud voices and laughter warming the house. Patrick had been putting in extra time with Mike over the last few weeks, needing to be ready for the camera in January, but he far preferred the time when they could all work out together.

"Hey, Emma," Mike said. "How's the shopping going?"

"Just when I think I'm done, I remember something else," she said. "How about you?"

"Nat has everything she could ever want or need," he said. "It's a little tough."

"I'm sure you'll think of something," Emma said.

"One year, I thought it was a great idea to give Kendra a coupon book," Dan said. "Unfortunately, she realized most of them benefited me. It didn't end well. She crossed out all

150

of the things I had written and replaced them with actual work. I had to repaint the bedrooms and wash dishes for almost a year. I do not recommend that."

"Mike's not an idiot," Jake said.

"Hey," Dan cried. "It's Christmas. You're supposed to be nice."

"Both of you need to play nice," Patrick said. "Or I'll tell Santa."

They all laughed as they pulled on jackets. "We'll see you tonight?" Jake asked, glancing between Patrick and Emma.

"I forgot to tell you," Patrick explained to her. "It's Christmas karaoke tonight. I told Jake that we would go. But if you're not up for it, we can skip."

"No, it sounds fun," Emma said. "I've been looking for an excuse to wear some of my Christmas outfits."

"Please tell me you got Patrick something to match," Dan said.

"You'll just have to wait and see," Emma said, grinning at them.

Once they had all left, Patrick turned to her with a pained look on his face. "You got me something hideous to wear, didn't you? Do I need to remind you how many pictures and videos are taken of me?"

"Not hideous," she promised. "Festive."

He groaned, and she laughed, then shrieked, as he picked her up and threw her over his shoulder. "I need your help showering if I'm going to be festive," he said as he carried her up the stairs.

***

When they arrived at the Windsor Palace, it was packed. There was a crowd waiting on the porch to get inside, so Patrick pulled into the small back parking lot, allowing them to enter through the kitchen. Zoe was in there and hugged both of them before gesturing to the door.

"You guys look amazing," Zoe said, glancing between them. Emma had found a cute little dress that alternated between red stripes with white snowflakes and white stripes covered with green Christmas trees. Patrick wore a matching sweater, which clung to his muscles in all the right places.

"Thanks," Patrick said, grinning at her. "I picked it all out."

Emma rolled her eyes. "He complained the whole way here."

"Kendra reserved your usual table for you," she said. "From what I've seen, your brothers are here, and JJ is with them. There's no sign of Nat and Mike, or Liam and Holly yet. You'll hear when they arrive, I'm sure. I'll be right out as soon as I help them catch up in here."

"Word must have gotten out that you'd be here," Emma said. The buzz in the kitchen was nothing compared to the roar of noise that hit them when they moved through the swinging door. At once, though, silence fell over the crowd as the local golden boy stepped into view. Within a few seconds, the locals went back to their conversations, but Emma could see some unfamiliar faces staring at them as they moved to

152

the table by the stage. Dan and Jake were at one end of the table, JJ at the other, so the three celebrities could sit in the middle. Patrick chose the seat next to Jake, with his back against the wall. The two men were the closest to the stage, which was appropriate since they would spend most of the night up there.

Within a few minutes, the noise level amped up again as Liam and Natalie entered through the front door. Mike led the way, his sheer size keeping the crowd back, as he led Natalie by the hand to the table. Liam's girlfriend Holly slipped past the crowd without anyone noticing, leaving the celebrities to pose for pictures.

"Hi," Holly said, sitting next to Emma. "Hopefully, he'll make his way here at some point."

"Desmond is watching from behind the bar," Emma told her. "He'll step in if need be."

"Oh, good," Holly said. "I wasn't able to see. I can't believe how crowded it is in here."

"I can't imagine why," Shea said with a laugh. "Not like we have three of the biggest names on the planet in the same room."

Kendra got on the stage after everyone had all settled in and ordered drinks. The crowd quieted when she tapped on the microphone, and she smiled out at them. "Welcome to the Palace," she said. "And Merry Christmas to you all. I know a lot of the faces in this room, and I appreciate all your support through the year. To our new friends, I hope you'll come back again. I'm officially opening the stage for Christmas Karaoke, and since I know it's what you all want, I'm going to invite my two favorite singers to the stage to kick us off. Jake and Patrick, will you do us the honors?"

The crowd went wild as the two brothers made their way up, and while they had a whispered discussion. Jake turned to tell the DJ what song they wanted to do, leaving Patrick to smile out at the crowd and wish them all a Merry Christmas. When the first tones of Mariah Carey's famous hit came over the speaker, the place erupted. Jake and Patrick split the lines up naturally, playing off each other as they went, until they finished with a bow.

"We don't want to hog the stage," Patrick said into the microphone. "Come on up and spread some cheer, and Jake and I will get back up in a little while. I'll let the DJ call the next singer."

The DJ took the microphone and called two women up, who rushed to the stage. Jake neatly put himself between them and Patrick, and their disappointed looks had Zoe nudging Emma. "Why do I think the only reason these two are performing was to get his attention?"

"I think it will be a long night of that," Emma replied. "But I just want to focus on the songs and being here with all of you."

"Same," Zoe said. "JJ and I talked to Maggie before we came over here. It sounds like she and Eve are fast friends already."

"Oh, I'm so relieved to hear that," Emma said. "I've been so worried. But I knew we were leaving her in the best possible place. Now I just need to see about contacting this long-lost aunt."

"Some people are lost because they want to be," Zoe said. "It worked out for us, and I hope the same will happen for her. But she needs to be prepared for the possibility that the aunt doesn't want her. And you should be as well."

"Maggie and Tim said she could stay with them no matter what," Emma said. "I'm torn between wanting that for her, and the mystery aunt. What if she goes with the aunt, and it's terrible?"

"Then she comes back," Zoe said. "There's no way Maggie would ever turn her away. But we'll cross that bridge if and when it comes. First, find the aunt and make sure she's legit. Don't let her catch on that you and Patrick are in any way involved in this. Then you'll know if she's coming for the right reasons. Do you need JJ's help?"

"Patrick hired a private investigator," Emma said. "I doubt anything will happen between now and Christmas, so I'll just try to put it out of my mind."

"Good." Zoe turned back to the stage as two singers finished a horrible but cheerful rendition of Deck the Halls. She clapped dutifully before turning back to Emma. "I'm just going to run to the kitchen and see what's taking our appetizers so long. I'll be right back."

When Zoe left the table, Emma was surprised that Jake moved over to take her seat. Of Patrick's family, he was the most reserved and hardest to get to know and rarely sought her out for a private conversation. It wasn't that he was rude, he was just very private. Emma knew he was still battling his issues from years in combat, so she didn't take it personally if he was quiet around her.

"Hey," Jake said. "Are you having fun?"

"I am," she said. "You and Patrick are the stars, of course. I can't imagine you'll be allowed to sit for much longer."

"No, we'll go back up in a minute," Jake said. "I wanted to ask you something first, if you don't mind."

"Of course, you can ask me anything."

"I got Patrick in the Secret Santa draw," Jake said. "I know I'm not supposed to tell anyone, but I'm stumped. He has everything he could ever want or need. What do I possibly get for him?"

"I was wondering who got him," Emma said with a laugh. "You're right, he does have everything he needs. Maybe there's something personal you could do? Something that would mean a lot to him on a sentimental level? I think that's what he loves the most anyway."

"Hmm, I hadn't thought of that," Jake said. "I'll give it some thought. If you think of anything he does need, will you let me know? Fancy socks or a new suitcase, whatever he might need before you guys leave."

"I'll give it some thought," Emma promised.

Patrick leaned across the table, looking between them. "If I could interrupt this weird meeting of the minds," he said, a teasing tone in his voice. "I think it's time to go up again."

Chapter 15

"What were you and Jake talking about?" Patrick asked, stealing Shea's seat while she was using the bathroom. He and Jake had been on stage for forty-five minutes, doing song after song, as everyone else in the room refused to replace them. Jake was setting up their guitars with the help of the DJ while Patrick sat for a break, so they could do some acoustic songs to end the night.

"Nothing much," Emma replied. "Just about Christmas."

"Really?" Patrick asked, feeling doubtful. "The two of you don't have many private conversations."

"He needed some gift ideas," Emma said. "For Shea. Just looking for a female perspective."

"Oh." Patrick looked over to where his brother was moving two stools onto the stage. "That's nice, that he thought to ask you. I like seeing you get closer to him."

"He's a hard nut to crack," Emma said. "He really didn't like me at first."

"I don't think that's true," Patrick said, thinking back to the early days. When Emma had first appeared, Jake had definitely put up more of a fuss than anyone else. "He was just being protective. That's who he is."

"I get it," Emma said. "No hard feelings, I promise. I just figured it's better to let him warm up to me than to push him for a friendship."

"That seems to be working," Patrick said. He leaned over and kissed her quickly. "A few more songs and we can go home. Any requests?"

"You know my favorites," Emma said. "And anything you sing will be perfect."

***

"What kind of ideas did Emma give you last night?" Patrick asked Jake as they stepped onto treadmills the next morning to warm up. Mike had insisted on keeping their workout schedule despite the late night before, because of the upcoming movie. Jake was the only other person to arrive so far, although Liam had texted that he was on his way.

"Ideas?" Jake asked, staring at the TV on the wall rather than meeting Patrick's eyes. "What do you mean?"

"When you asked her about gifts for Shea," Patrick said.

"Oh, that."

"Did you have another conversation that I missed?" Patrick snapped, unsure why his brother was being cagey.

Jake glanced over at Patrick. "Don't get mad."

"I'm not," Patrick said with a sigh. "I'm exhausted and stressed. And I thought this would be an easy question. I just wanted a simple answer so I could move on to asking for help with my issue."

"It is, sorry," Jake said. "I'm tired too. What are you trying to figure out?"

"I've gotten a bunch of things for Emma so far," Patrick said. "But I feel like I'm missing something. I thought maybe if she told you what to get for Shea, it might help me know what she'd like."

Jake raised his speed so that he was at a slight jog as he answered. "She told me to give from the heart," he said. "Something that will have an emotional connection. It was good advice."

"I should have thought of that," Patrick said. He pushed the button to match his brother's speed, laughing when Jake immediately sped up. "Of course, she would want something special that money can't buy. Now I just need to figure out what that is."

"Do you have any pictures of her mom?" Mike asked from across the room where he was setting up the weights. "She was talking to Nat the other day about how the holidays were a special time for them. Maybe you could do something with that?"

"That's a good idea," Patrick said. His brain started working a mile a minute, running through ideas.

"And you need to do it yourself," Jake said. "Don't outsource it to someone else. Have it be from you."

"Easier said than done," Patrick said. "I'm not super creative. I might need help if it's something made. But I'll come up with the idea on my own."

"Good plan," Jake said.

"What plan?" Liam's voice called out as he came into the gym.

"We were talking about Christmas presents," Patrick replied. "What did you get for Holly?"

"I struggled," Liam said. "She keeps saying she doesn't need anything. And yet she is the most Christmas-y person I know, so I need to hit it out of the park."

"What did you end up doing?" Jake asked.

"I adopted the pediatric wing at a hospital for the holiday, in her name," Liam answered. "I know she doesn't want to be caught on camera, so I arranged to have the toys delivered and a video made for her."

"That's amazing," Patrick said.

"I am," Liam said. When they all laughed, he grinned. "I mean, yes, it is. And I also booked us a charter yacht in the Mediterranean for a week."

"Do you mean you bought yourself a yacht?" Patrick asked, teasing his friend.

"I thought about it," Liam said. "But my money man suggested renting first to make sure we even like it."

"Mike, what are you giving Nat?" Patrick asked, noticing his friend had been quieter than usual.

"I was going to propose," he said. "I've had the ring for so long now, and her dad already gave me his permission. But then she mentioned that she wouldn't want something like that to happen right before she starts to film. Said it would put even more attention on her, and us, and it would take away from her being able to enjoy it."

"Well, that complicates things," Liam said. "But I get it. We're followed nonstop, and people are always trying to get pictures of us on set."

"What's the backup plan?" Patrick asked.

"I don't have one," Mike said. "That's the problem."

"I'm guessing a yacht is out of the question," Liam said. When Mike scowled at him, he laughed and threw his hands up. "Only kidding."

"My sister is coming to town this weekend," Mike said. "My whole family is coming for the week of Christmas, but she's coming early to help me."

"The lovely Stassi," Liam said. "It will be nice to see her again."

"You're in a committed relationship," Mike snapped at him.

"I know, I know," Liam said. "And I meant her personality. You all know how happy I am with Holly. I'd never do anything to ruin that. I don't miss the bachelor days."

"Speaking of, is Zane still planning to come here so we can all fly together?" Patrick asked, referring to their fourth co-star. Zane was still living the single life, flying from city to city and relishing the attention from fans.

"He says he is, but who knows," Liam said. "His family wants him to come home, but he said since we'll be shooting over there, he'll have enough time with them. He wanted to spend Christmas on a beach, last I heard."

"I'm sure our version of New Year's Eve would be too boring for him," Jake said. "I'll be surprised if he comes."

"It's going to be weird when you're all gone," Jake said. "Just me and Dan left behind. I don't know if we'll survive it."

"JJ will be here too," Patrick said.

"True," Jake said. "He'll keep us in line."

"I'll be back and forth," Mike added. "When I need to check in with the gym. I think the manager has it under control, and I spend less time there now than ever, but you never know."

"I'm hoping we're back by spring," Liam said. "I won't mind leaving for the coldest part of the year, but I'd rather not be gone more than six months."

"Same," Patrick said. "That's what I've heard. Six months now, and then reshoots and voiceovers over the next year or so."

"Works for me," Liam said. "Holly is going to enjoy some time off, and she wants to be back by the time Shea has the baby."

"Will she come back early?" Jake asked.

"Yes. She knows that you guys will need help with Charlie and Izzie, and she wants to do that," Liam said. "Plus, I tend to get cranky over the last few weeks of filming, so she's happy to head back."

"Just the last few weeks?" Patrick teased his friend. "All it takes is one bad craft service spread, and you're miserable for a week."

"Is it so much to ask that we have something I like?"

"It's not the catering company's fault that you don't like healthy food," Patrick pointed out.

"So many vegetables. It's enough to ruin a man's day."

"What I hear you saying is that you need to run more," Mike said. "Work off all those junk food calories you're taking in."

"Hey, it's Christmas! Aren't we supposed to be eating cookies and drinking the nog?" Liam yelled as Mike turned up the speed on his machine.

****

"How was your workout?" Emma was sitting on the couch, a cup of tea in her hand, staring at the Christmas tree as she asked.

"It was good," he said. "What are you up to?"

"I just talked to Maggie," she said. "Eve is doing good. They're even making cookies to enter into tonight's contest."

"I almost forgot that we were judging that, until Mike made me burn an extra five hundred calories to compensate," he said. "I probably should have a light dinner."

"You know you don't have to eat the entire cookie, right?"

"It feels rude not to," he explained. "Have you ever seen Santa not finish the cookie?"

She laughed and put the mug of tea down as she stood and stretched. "I have some more wrapping to do," she said. "Do you have anything to add to the pile?"

"You've been on top of it," he said. "Thanks for doing all the kids' presents."

"I think you bought out the entire doll section for Calle," she said with a laugh. "And I don't think Charlie needed three hockey sticks."

"You'd be surprised. They break easier than they should," he said. "That reminds me, I want to book them for a weekend in Boston for a Bruins game."

"Is that your way of telling me you got Jake in the family exchange?"

"No," he said. "It's a gift for Charlie. This was my way around the rules," he said. "I got things for the kids that the parents can enjoy as well."

"They're going to be mad," she said.

"No, they won't," he said. "It's the one time a year that I can pamper my family without them feeling weird about it."

"Did you get something extra for the person you chose in the exchange?"

"Is that your way of asking who I got?" He couldn't help teasing her and laughed when she blushed.

"Busted," she said. "I am curious, but it adds to the fun."

"Do you want me to tell you?"

"No," she said. "I'm having too much fun trying to figure it out. And I finally thought of the perfect gift for my person, so I don't need to ask for help."

"Okay, if you're all set, I'm going to head into my office for a bit," he said. "I need to call Sean and work on a few things."

"Tell him I said hi," she said, spreading out the wrapping paper on the coffee table. "I'm going to put on White Christmas on TV and take care of all the last few gifts."

He slid his AirPods in once he was settled behind his desk, hitting Sean's name on his phone screen to dial. His assistant answered on the first ring, as usual. "Hey, boss man," he said. "What can I do for you?"

"I'm not supposed to ask for help, according to my brothers," he said. "But I had an idea for Emma's Christmas present, and I wondered if you could get me some phone numbers."

"Absolutely," he said. "What are you looking for?"

"I have some pictures that Emma has of her and her mom, and some from when her mom was younger," he said. "Plus, she has a few recordings with her mom's voice on them. Obviously, these are prized possessions, so I need to make sure they get into the right hands. But I need help to make a video for her and preserve them so they'll last forever."

"I know just the guy," Sean said. "And he happens to live in New York. I could arrange for him to come to you, so it will be done without having to ship anything."

"That would be amazing," Patrick said. "Should I call him first?"

"Let me call him first and set everything up, and then you can talk about what you want when he arrives," San responded. "Luckily for you, I have all the rooms at the Inn booked, so I don't need to worry about where he's going to stay."

"Great," Patrick said. "I knew I could count on you."

"Always," Sean said. "I'll text you shortly with his info and when he'll be arriving."

"Are you sure he'll be able to come here at the drop of a hat?"

"For you? Positive," Sean said. "He's new to the scene, but I know him personally and trust him. The opportunity to work with you, even on a small project, would have him walking to Vermont."

"Well, let's get him on a plane," Patrick said, laughing. "If he were to walk, he wouldn't arrive until after Christmas."

"He'll be there with plenty of time," Sean assured him. "Anything else?"

"No, thanks," Patrick said, ending the call. He scrolled through his contacts to find the number of the private investigator he had called about Eve and hit the number to call him.

"Edward Ruiz," he answered, his voice crisp and authoritative. He had worked as a Boston police detective when JJ was on the force and had come through for Patrick in the past.

"Edward, it's Patrick Burrows. I just wanted to check on the woman you were looking into for me."

"Hey, Patrick. I have some news, but I'm not sure how good it is," Edward said. "Tori Rogers lives in Tennessee right now, but she was originally from upstate New York, where Eve first went into foster care. She doesn't have any children and works as a waitress. I'm not sure she's the motherly type, I have to say. I managed to chat with her a few times at her work and talked to some of her co-workers. She's a loner, keeps to herself. Told me she has never had kids. She lives alone in a one-bedroom apartment, drives a beat-up car. Looks down on her luck."

"Shoot. A part of me was hoping she was a mom, or was actively looking for her lost niece," Patrick said. "What now?"

"You have two choices," Edward said. "I can talk to her privately, explain the situation. See if she'd be open to changing her life. Or I can walk away."

"We can't do that," Patrick said. "This is the only family member we know about for this kid. She needs to at least have a chance at connecting. Let me think for a minute."

Edward sat in silence while Patrick's mind ran through all the options. Finally thinking of the best solution for everyone, at least as far as he could tell, he sent a text before starting to explain to Edward. When the response came through immediately, he felt like it was a sign he was making the right decision. Now it was out of his hands, and he could say he had done everything possible to help Eve.

Chapter 16

"I don't even understand how so many people are so talented in the kitchen, and I can barely make a chocolate chip cookie," Emma said as she walked through the high school gymnasium with Kendra and Shea. The room was lined with tables of local bakers, who had all entered the Christmas Cookie Contest. Patrick was on the stage, along with Liam and Natalie, as the local celebrity judges. Rounding out the panel were Piper, who owned the bakery, Stella Burrows and Zoe.

Kendra nodded as she looked around the busy room. "It's grown every year. But now, having three celebrity judges is really bringing in everyone within driving distance. I spoke to one woman who even came in from seven hours away."

"Wow," Emma said. "That's commitment. I hope she gets to meet whoever she came for."

"You know they'll all go out of their way to talk to everyone," Kendra said. "How are you doing on your holiday shopping?"

"Every time I think I'm done, I find more to buy," Emma said with a laugh. "How about you?"

"Same," Kendra said. "We had to tell Calle that Santa's deadline has passed for new wish lists. She comes up with ten more things every day."

"It's hard to believe it's almost here," Emma said. "I always wish that the season lasted longer. It goes by way too fast."

"I agree, but the prep work is so exhausting," Shea said. "I'm looking forward to when it's finally Christmas Eve, and I can just relax."

"Are you sure you're okay to do both Christmas Eve and day at our house?" Emma asked. "I feel bad dragging you all out two days in a row."

"Are you kidding? We don't have to clean, or stress about what a mess is made opening gifts. Coming to your house is a luxury," Shea replied. "As long as you don't mind?"

"Not at all," Emma assured her. "Palace Plates is supplying all the food, so I don't have to stress. And we want to soak up every minute of family time before we leave."

"We'll all miss you," Kendra said. "It will be weird without you guys here for a few months."

"I know, it will be weird for us too," Emma said.

"No luck with planning the wedding before you leave?" Shea asked.

"It's kind of shifted to the back burner," Emma said. "It's been a little crazier than usual lately. And we don't want to try to squeeze it in while he's filming."

"I'm sorry. I know you were excited about it," Shea said.

"I still am. It will just be a little longer than we had expected, which is okay. If life has taught me anything, it's that things won't go according to plan. I need to make the best of what I have and be happy with it. I have a man I love, who loves me back, a roof over my head, and a new family," Emma said. "I have everything I ever dreamed of."

"We're so lucky to have you a part of the family," Kendra said, linking her arm with Emma's on one side and Shea on the other. "The three of us Burrows wives have a lot to live up to, with the standards that Stella set. But I think we're up for it. And we have a major advantage."

"What's that?" Emma asked.

"Each other," Kendra said with a laugh. "Who else could relate?"

***

"I never want to eat another cookie," Patrick said with a moan, laying down on the couch.

"I'll make you a cup of tea," Emma said, laughing. "Mike told you to take one small bite, not eat the whole thing."

"Liam was eating the whole cookie," Patrick said. "How would it have looked if I had only taken one bite?"

"Nat managed just fine," Emma said. "Barely a nibble."

"She's so much smarter than us," Patrick said. "Always has been. Don't tell her I said that."

"I think she already knows," Emma said. "I guess we don't need to worry about dinner tonight?"

"Tonight? I'll never eat again," Patrick said. "Can we just relax tonight? Watch a movie and let my digestive system recover?"

171

"Absolutely," Emma said. "But I'm going to eat popcorn, so prepare yourself."

"I might have to tell Santa you're being mean," Patrick said, making her laugh. "Your stocking might be full of coal."

"I somehow doubt that," Emma said, handing him the tea. "Santa has too big a heart to ever do something like that."

"You're right. And you're so good ninety-nine percent of the time," Patrick said. "I'm sure he'll forgive this one moment of cruelty."

"Is this a bad time to tell you that I bought three dozen cookies today?" Emma said, teasing him. "They all looked so amazing as you ate them, I couldn't resist."

"Oh, I'm definitely telling Santa on you," Patrick said.

"Speaking of Santa," Emma said, settling onto the couch next to him. "I was talking to Kendra and Shea today about Christmas. I think we're all set to host, right?"

"As far as I know," Patrick replied. "All the food is ordered. I have a cleaning service coming on the twenty-third, so we don't have to stress. And I think we're done shopping and wrapping, unless I'm mistaken?"

"No, I think we're done," Emma said. "I just feel like I'm missing something."

"It's been an emotional week for you," Patrick said. "The whole month, really. We tried and failed to pull off a wedding before we leave, and I know that's disappointing. You're missing your mom, and everything with Eve brought back a lot. I think it's normal to feel the way you are feeling."

"You know I'm okay about the wedding. I don't want to do it if we can't have it be perfect, and just for us," she said. "But speaking of Eve, have you heard anything from the private investigator?"

"He's still working on it," Patrick said. "I hope to hear more soon."

"I don't know what to hope for," Emma said, her mind running with the possibilities. "Ideally, everything will go well, and she'd be happy with her aunt. But I would be nervous, sending her off to live somewhere new, where we can't see how she's doing. What if it's a disaster, and we don't know because she's in some far-off city?"

"I agree," Patrick said. "We'll find a way to make it work. I promise."

"Did you see her today? She was with the Monahans, and she was glowing," Emma said. "She's met some other kids in town and is actually excited about starting school here after the break."

"Speaking of the Monahans, I was trying to think of something to order and send to their house for the holidays," Patrick said. "As a thank you for opening their home to Eve. But I know Zoe will handle all the food, and it looked like they had every possible Christmas decoration. Any ideas?"

"What about some Christmas breakfast items? Zoe will make all the food for the dinners, and for appetizers, but I don't think they'll plan ahead for that," Emma said after a moment's thought. "Piper was putting together fruit and pastry trays for families to pick up, maybe we could do one of those?"

"Perfect," Patrick said. "I'll pop in there and organize it."

Emma laughed. "Based on the crowd today, I think you should leave it to me."

"As long as you're sure? I know it's been hard, worrying about the press sneaking up on you," Patrick said.

"I do feel like we should just get ahead of it," Emma said. "Can we just make an announcement? Maybe do one photoshoot, just to get it over with?"

"Are you sure? Missy started pushing for that right away, but I was saying no. Especially because she had convinced me it was a better idea to wait until the negative stories had died down. And now this will make you even more of a public figure," Patrick said. "And it means we'll be tracked everywhere we go, because they'll be on wedding watch."

"I know," Emma said with a sigh. "But being suspicious of every new face, and wearing gloves everywhere I go, is getting old. We should be celebrating this time of our lives, and instead we're hiding it. It makes me feel like we're ashamed, or something."

"You're absolutely right," Patrick said. "I wasn't trying to hide it because I wasn't proud of our relationship. Or of you, for that matter. I thought I was doing the right thing to protect you. But I would much rather shout from the rooftops that you're mine, that you said yes, and then we can deal with whatever comes."

"We'll be in it together," Emma said. "And once we're on location, we're going to be living under a spotlight, anyway. This way, we can control a tiny bit of it. If we go public and give an interview and some pictures, it will be hard to say that we're in this for any reason other than love. As long as we get someone who has been positive and supportive, not one who keeps trying to tear us down."

"Do you have a preference of who we talk to?"

"You pick," Emma said. "You know them better than I do, and Missy pays attention to who gives us favorable angles. I trust your judgement."

"Okay, I'll make some calls in the morning," he said. "If that's okay. Right now, I want to cuddle up with you and watch a corny movie."

"Corny?" she said with fake outrage as she reached for the remote. "Now you're in for it. I was going to go easy on you with a comedy, but now I think we need a classic."

***

Within two days, Hollywood arrived in Vermont. Patrick's trusted stylist, Maria, flew in first, with two assistants and a plane full of clothes. Emma barely had a chance to say hello to them before she was being led to the center of the room, surrounded by racks of dresses and outfits.

"We have very little time," Maria said, looking Emma up and down. "Thank goodness you are easy to dress. Now, let's get going."

Emma laughed and let the assistant help her get the first dress over her head, then zipped up. The dress fit like a second skin, a gorgeous emerald color that clung to her curves and left little to the imagination.

175

"No, not right," Maria said. "Too much. Let's try the next."

Dress after dress was pulled out, with Maria rejecting each one. A few she put aside for future events, declaring them right for the Oscars or a red carpet, but not a photoshoot. When the assistant came toward her with a red dress, Emma shook her head.

"No, not red," she said. "I never wear it."

"We'll see about that," Maria said, gesturing for the assistant to proceed. The dress slipped over her head, and with a soft swish, fell to the floor. Although the color was bright, the dress was shockingly simple. A scoop neckline with just enough extra material to swoop, spaghetti straps, and soft silk down to her ankles. Maria stopped back with a satisfied look on her face. "This is it."

"No, it can't be," Emma said. "Red says look at me."

"My darling," Maria said with a laugh. "Trust me when I say, there is no escaping everyone looking at you. You're going to be on the cover of a magazine. On the social media. Blasted around the world minutes after the photos are taken. It's too late to worry about people looking at you."

"I just mean, Patrick is the star," she said. "He should be the focus."

"He will look dashing in a black tuxedo with some red highlights," Maria said. "We can have your hair put up, some festive greenery maybe to add to the holiday look. No jewelry other than the ring. It's perfect."

"You know what people will say," Emma said, trying again. "They'll say I'm trying to steal the spotlight. People will hate this."

"I've been working in this industry for longer than you've been alive," Maria said. "Know what I've learned?"

"What?"

"No one outside of your house matters," Maria said. "If you wouldn't invite them in for coffee, you don't let their opinion shape how you view yourself."

"That's really good advice," Emma admitted.

"Good, now that we know I'm always right, let's move on to the next," Maria said.

"This was all I needed today," Emma said, confused.

"You need a wedding dress," Maria said, winking at her. "You think I didn't come prepared?"

"But we don't even have a date yet."

"You won't be able to try on dresses once the news gets out," Maria said. "The only way to choose one and have it stay private is to do it now."

The doorbell rang, and one of the assistants opened it to reveal Zoe, Stella, Shea and Kendra. They all looked confused when they saw who was in the room but came in when Maria beckoned them.

"Come in, come in," she said. "We're just getting to the good stuff."

"Patrick texted," Zoe said to Emma. "Asked us to come over, said you needed us?"

"I told him to, because she does," Maria answered for her. "Although he doesn't know why, he thinks they're here to give their opinion on your photoshoot outfit. But no one should try on wedding dresses without their family, so it was worth the little deception. Sit, we'll be right back."

The other women erupted in cheers as Emma followed Maria into the next room, where more racks were set up. White dresses filled the room, bringing Emma to a stop. The reality of what she was about to do sank in, and she battled with her emotions. Even though Patrick had thought of having her sister, and her new family, there with her, she couldn't help but think of what her own mother was missing.

Maria was busy fussing with the dresses, choosing one off the rack to look at, her back to Emma. "I don't get to do this often," she said. "I tend to do more red-carpet events than weddings, but for you, I wanted to be the one to help. I lost my own mother young, and I know how you're feeling."

Emma swallowed a knot in her throat, tears shimmering and making it difficult to see the small woman as she turned around, a white dress in hand. She was overcome, making it hard to find her voice, but Maria didn't seem as if she was looking for an answer.

"She's here, you know," Maria said softly. "I can feel her, right here, watching you. Love never dies. It stays in your heart, and she gets to be with you everywhere you go. If you love Christmas as much as Patrick says, you'll let yourself feel the magic of the season bringing your mom to you right now."

Emma was shocked when Maria pulled her in for a tight, fast hug, before clearing her throat and getting down to business. She gestured for Emma to remove the red dress, which she carefully hung back up before helping her step into the white concoction on the floor. Emma let herself be led back out to the living room, where the other women all gasped and stood to fuss over her. Although she hadn't even seen the dress in the mirror yet, she felt like a bride for the first time. And it was a feeling she would savor.

Chapter 17

The photoshoot took place on the twenty-second, and within hours, the pictures had hit the internet and gone viral. Patrick had sat on a club chair in his own living room, Emma draped across his lap in a red dress that was made straight from his dreams. They had then posed in front of their Christmas tree, the fireplace, and taken a final shot under the mistletoe. In that one, the photographer had Emma slip off her high heels and dangle them from one finger, while Patrick had removed his tux jacket, untied the bow tie and unbuttoned most of his shirt. They stood, lips a breath away from each other, until the photographer had declared it perfect.

"Dude, you're burning up the internet," Liam had declared when he arrived for a workout. "That last picture? Hot."

Patrick shook his head to clear out the thoughts of what had happened between him and Emma minutes after the door closed behind the photographer, when he'd been able to show her exactly what the dress had done to him for hours. "I'm trying to avoid looking," he said. "Or at least, avoid the comments."

"I'm sure it's as brutal as ever," Liam said cheerfully. "But who cares? You're living your life, not theirs."

"I just don't want it to ruin Emma's Christmas."

"Then don't let it," Liam said. "Distract her. Throw away the phones, turn off the Wi-Fi. Whatever you need to do."

"Are you still coming here to spend the day with us?"

"Christmas? Yeah," Liam said. "Holly is excited. We both are."

"Nat and Mike are having his family," Patrick said. "They'll all stop by on Christmas Eve, along with the Monahans, but on Christmas Day it will be just us."

"Sounds like you have a lot to do," Liam said. "I'm happy that all I need to do is show up with a smile on my face."

"Show up where?" Mike asked as he walked through the front door and pulled off his coat.

"Here, for Christmas," Liam said. "Patrick has to do all the work to host for the day. I just get to eat, drink and be merry."

"More merry, less eating and drinking," Mike said. "You're nowhere near ready for the movie."

"What do you mean?" Liam cried, looking down at himself. "I look better than Patrick."

"Absolutely not," Mike said. "Patrick has been working hard. You're two weeks from being on camera, and you're going to need them to paint on abs for you."

"You're cruel," Liam said. "I'm in love. Maybe I eat a little more chocolate, just because I'm so happy."

"The two don't have to go hand in hand," Mike said. They all started walking down the stairs to the gym, with the trainer in the lead. "Nat's in love, and she eats plenty of lettuce."

"It's so boring," Liam said, his tone whiny. "Why can't lettuce taste better? It's so blah."

"Talk to me about boring when you get to Scotland and nothing fits," Mike said. "Did you see how Patrick looked in those pictures? You need to get there."

"You looked at the gossip rags?" Patrick asked, surprised.

"Not so much looked as was shown," Mike said. "You guys looked great. Nat was impressed."

"If you want to pop the question and take the heat off me, I wouldn't be upset," Patrick said.

"Really?" Mike stopped what he was doing and stared at Patrick. "You don't want me to give you some time?"

"Time for more scrutiny? Absolutely not," Patrick said. "And there is no way I'd ever want you to delay your happiness for my sake. That's not what you're doing, is it?"

Mike shrugged. "No. Nat and I talked about it, and I was right that she didn't want me to do it before the movie films. She's under enough stress during filming, and us getting engaged would just put her even more under the microscope. She'd rather I wait until we're back here and things are quiet."

"Do things ever get quiet?" Patrick asked, glancing between Mike and Liam. "Don't delay your happiness because of the expectations of the world. I learned that myself recently."

Mike fiddled with the weights and didn't answer, causing Liam and Patrick to exchange a look. Liam laughed, breaking the tension, and pointed at Mike. "You're making me delay my happiness."

"You're going to propose?" Patrick looked at his friend in surprise.

"Well, sure, one day," Liam said. "But I meant Mike. He wants me on a diet at the best time of the year."

"Asking you to eat a little less and work out a little more so I don't look like a failure at my job is not the same," Mike said, rolling his eyes.

***

When his phone rang toward the end of their workout, Patrick ignored Mike's look and stepped out to answer. The incoming call from the private investigator was worth an extra ten minutes on the treadmill later. "Edward, hi," he said.

"Morning, Patrick," he said. "I'm sorry this has taken longer than I thought it would. But I've got good news."

"Really?"

"Yes," he said. "I met with Tori yesterday, and we went over everything. She was shocked to find out that she has a niece but admitted that she's not sure she would be in a position to care for someone. Especially a kid she's never met. But when I told her the plan you came up with, she agreed to it. She had a lot of questions, but I kept your name out of it and made sure she was doing it for the kid."

"When will she arrive?"

"She's going to start driving today," Edward said. "Should be there on Christmas Eve, if the weather holds out."

"What's your feeling on this? Will it work out?"

184

"She asked if I knew what the girl would like for Christmas," Edward said. "That's a good sign. She's a hard worker, liked by her neighbors and coworkers, even though she keeps to herself. My instincts say that she's a good person who has had a rough life and finds it hard to trust. I don't think she would commit to coming there just to let the girl down."

"Good," Patrick said, relief coursing through his body. "I've been so nervous about this."

"Happy to help," Edward said. "If that's all, I'm going to head home. My wife is anxious for me to be back for the holidays."

"Let me know if you have any issues with flights, and I'll take care of it," Patrick said. "And I'll arrange to send something nice to your wife as a thank you."

"Not necessary, but she would appreciate it," Edward said.

"And you'll send your invoice over to Sean?"

"I'll get it to him tomorrow," Edward said. "Have a Merry Christmas."

"You as well," Patrick said, hanging up. He wandered back into the gym, where Liam was flat on his back on the floor and Mike was standing over him laughing.

"He's trying to kill me," Liam said.

"I'm going to leave you to it," Patrick replied. "Mike, I'll make up the time later, I swear. But I have to talk to Emma about something important."

"Want us to head out?" Liam asked, sounding hopeful.

"No, you're good," Patrick said, already heading for the stairs. "She's out in the stable, so I'll be out there."

He pulled on a jacket before running out the kitchen door toward the stable. Emma typically helped with the horses each morning or took videos to post on the rescue's social media. It had been extremely helpful in finding them new, safe homes, and she took pride in it. When his eyes adjusted to the dimmer light in the stable, he saw that was exactly what she was doing, so he waited for her to finish before clearing his throat.

"Hey," she said, smiling at him. "You're done early."

"Because I just got really good news, and I had to tell you right away." He led her to a small table at the end of the stable, where the staff who managed the horses could eat their lunch or enjoy a cup of coffee.

"Tell me," she said, looking at him expectantly.

"I didn't want to get your hopes up, but Edward found Eve's aunt a few days ago," he said. "Don't be mad at me for not telling you. I knew it would crush you if things went bad."

"Which means they went well?"

"It did," he said. "Tori Richards is a single woman who has been living in Nashville. She was waiting tables and living alone. According to her neighbors and coworkers, she's a hard worker and keeps to herself. Edward and I had talked about what the best approach would be, given what we knew."

"Okay," Emma said, waving a hand for him to move on.

"I asked him to feel her out about taking custody of Eve but offer another possibility if she was reluctant. When he told her that she had a niece, she was shocked," Patrick said. "She had no idea. But she was overwhelmed at what that meant, and uncomfortable being thrust into a parent role."

"Can't blame her for that," Emma said softly. "I'm sure it was a shock."

"I had talked to Piper about her desperate need for help at the bakery," Patrick continued. "I asked if she would consider hiring Eve's aunt, assuming she was willing to move here. I even offered to pay her salary, on the down low. But she said she'd be happy to hire her if she had experience in food service, which she does. The plan is for her to move here, work for Piper, and get to know Eve while she's still living with the Monahans. That way, we know Eve is safe and happy, but she'll have her aunt in her life."

"Where will she live?"

"I rented her a small house on Oak Street," he said. "It was empty but furnished, and the owner was more than happy to let her move in when she arrived. I told Edward to tell her it's a perk of the job, and Piper agreed to go along with it."

"I'm not sure I like deceiving her," Emma said.

"I agree, but it's necessary for now," Patrick said. "My name couldn't be a part of this. The last thing we needed was this woman showing up thinking she can get close to me, or get something from me. This way, she's coming for Eve, and not for any other reason."

"When will you tell Eve? And Maggie and Tim?"

"She's going to be here tomorrow," Patrick said. "If all goes well on the drive."

"Christmas Eve, and Eve gets a family," Emma said with a smile. "Kind of perfect."

"It's also Eve's birthday, so it really is," Patrick said.

"That's right, I almost forgot," Emma said. "Should we tell her in the morning? Kind of a birthday present?"

"Perfect," Patrick said. "I love that my future wife is so smart."

"And I love that you're so caring," she said, moving to sit on his lap. She kissed him, then put her head on his chest. "Thank you for doing this."

"I'll do anything for you."

"I know," she said, looking up at him with a smile. "That's why I'm going to ask to exploit you. Will you take a picture with Whiskers? He's been with us for a few months, and he needs to find his forever home now that he's done with his training. A picture with you will get him lots of attention."

"Pictures of me with a Santa hat," he said, spotting the prop on the counter where she had set her stuff down. "Even better."

***

Patrick woke up alone early on Christmas Eve and followed the smell of coffee to find Emma sitting by the

Christmas tree. "Good morning," he said, leaning down to kiss her softly. "Merry Christmas Eve."

"You too," she said, smiling up at him. "I was too excited to sleep. I hope I'm not too tired later to wait up for Santa."

"I'll keep you awake," he promised. "What do we need to do before everyone else arrives?"

"Not much," she said. "The house is clean, and all the food was delivered yesterday. I was just thinking about maybe setting up some of the games now, but that was just to kill time until you woke up. Or until it's a reasonable time to go to the Monahans."

"I doubt it's ever too early to knock on their door," Patrick said with a laugh. "But I'll text JJ and ask."

Within a few minutes, his phone dinged with a reply. "JJ says his parents are up with the sun," he said. "They won't think it's unusual if we go early. Maybe we can bring some breakfast for everyone?"

"Good idea," Emma said, jumping to her feet. "I'm going to go crazy if I sit here for one more minute."

Within an hour, they were both showered and in the car, heading through town. The lights were on the big tree in the town square and twinkled on every surface as they drove. The town was more than ready for Santa to arrive, and it put Patrick in an even better mood. Once they had picked up a breakfast quiche from Piper and a tray full of hot cocoa and coffee to go along with the food, they pulled into the Monahans' driveway. Smoke billowed out of the chimney, and the lights were on, so it was evident they weren't waking anyone up.

Emma looked at Patrick nervously as they rang the doorbell. "I hope she's happy with this," she whispered.

"I know," Patrick said. "If she's not, we'll figure it out."

Tim Monahan opened the door, a smile on his face. "Merry Christmas," he said. "What a treat this is."

"We come bearing food and hot drinks," Patrick said, holding up the offerings. "If you and Maggie have a minute to talk. And Eve, if she's awake?"

"She is," Tim said. "She and Maggie are busy baking in the kitchen. I feel like I live in a cookie warehouse now. Come on in."

"Well, good morning," Maggie called out. "And Merry Christmas! I didn't think we would see you until we stopped by tonight."

"We have some news," Patrick said. Eve's smile slipped, a wary look coming onto her face at his words. "Good news, I think. Should we all sit?"

They all gathered around the table, and Patrick quickly outlined what Edward had found out about Tori, and what the plan was. Eve visibly relaxed once he had finished, and he noticed she had been holding Maggie's hand.

"Does that mean I can stay here?" Eve asked, her voice tremulous.

"Yes," Patrick said. "As long as that's alright with all of you? I thought it might be easier for you to get to know your aunt if you weren't trying to also live together. And that being here, in Windsor Peak, we can all keep an eye on things."

"Is it okay with you both?" Eve asked, her eyes darting between Maggie and Tim. "If I stay?"

"Of course," Maggie said quickly, Tim nodding at the same time. "We told you that you'd always have a place here. Nothing will change that. And we're not ready to let you go, if we're being honest."

"Are you sure?" Eve wiped quickly at her cheek, and Patrick realized she was crying.

"Honey, I know we're not your parents," Tim said. "But it's an honor to be able to stand in their place. You're a part of our family now."

"You're so much better than my parents," Eve said, the tears now fully falling. "I was so afraid I would have to leave. I wanted to find my aunt, but then I was scared. I really like it here, and I didn't want to leave you guys. Or Windsor Peak, right when I was starting to feel normal. I even have some friends here."

"And now you have the best of both worlds, thanks to Patrick and Emma," Maggie said, beaming at him. "This is the best Christmas present ever."

"I'm glad we could help," Patrick said. "We'll let you get back to your baking, and we'll see you later."

He watched as Emma and Eve hugged, and whispered words to each other. Emma had been strangely quiet during the whole exchange, and he was worried about her. But seeing her smile at the young girl, he realized she had been nervous about what her reaction would be. Seeing that she was happy now, and could really enjoy Christmas with this weight lifted, filled him with joy.

Chapter 18

By late afternoon, Emma and Patrick were ready for their family and friends to arrive. Patrick had showered again and changed into a pair of jeans and a light-up reindeer sweater, while she had opted for a simple green dress. When she had tried to leave the bedroom, he had handed her the cardigan he had purchased for her, with a light-up Christmas tree on the back. Fortunately, it matched her dress, she thought as she pulled it on. And she owed him after the outfit he wore to Christmas karaoke.

The doorbell rang as they were walking down the stairs together, and within minutes, the house was full of laughter and hugs as the Burrows family piled in. Calle zipped around the room, inspecting presents and the stockings hanging on the chimney before cornering Patrick.

"Uncle Patty, we have a problem," she said, hands on her hips.

Patrick crouched down to be at eye level with her. "What is it?"

"Santa can't come down the chimney if you have a fire," she said. "We need to put it out."

"But we don't have any kids here," he said. "I don't think Santa needs to visit us."

"You have stockings," she said indignantly, pointing. "Who else would fill them?"

"You're absolutely right," Patrick said, meeting Emma's eyes. "We'll make sure to cool it off with plenty of time, okay?"

Appeased, Calle raced back across the room to grab Charlie, dragging him to the pile of presents under the tree. Patrick made his way to Emma's side, where she had given in to her laughter.

"I guess I need to get better at this stuff before we have kids," he said.

"Good thing we have some time," she said. "She had you on your heels."

"Not too much time, though, okay?" Patrick kissed her on the head as the doorbell rang again. "I can't wait too long to see you as a mom."

She watched as he crossed the room to open the door for JJ and Zoe, followed by the Monahan family. Eve was the last to enter, pulled into the room by Maggie. Emma made her way over to say hello, catching Eve as she took off her coat.

"Merry Christmas," she said, giving her a quick hug. "And happy birthday again!"

"Thanks," Eve said with a shy smile. "This is the best one I've had in years."

"I'm sure," Emma said. "Did you have a chance to meet your aunt?"

Eve shook her head. "She got caught up in bad weather, I guess. She called and talked to Maggie for a little while. Hopefully, she will make it tomorrow, but she thought it would be better to let me have Christmas without worrying about meeting her. So, we'll meet on the twenty-sixth."

"You're okay with that?"

"Yes," Eve said. "I want her to get here safely. And I also don't want anything to ruin today and tomorrow. You know?"

"I do," Emma said. "But I think it's going to go well. It means something that she was willing to pack up her whole life and move here. try to think positive, okay?"

Eve nodded, and Emma pulled her further into the room with her. After introducing her to Charlie and Calle, she felt safe leaving her in the company of the kids. Spotting Zoe in the kitchen, she made her way to her sister's side.

"Hey," she said. "Shouldn't you be taking it easy?"

"There's a doctor and a nurse in the house," Zoe said, pointing to her sister-in-law Finley and her fiancé, Evan. "And I've been told that it's good to stay active. I feel good, the baby is doing well."

"Can you believe that next year, you'll be a mom?" Emma clapped her hands. "I can't believe you'll have a baby by next Christmas."

"No," Zoe said, shaking her head. "It's still hard to wrap my head around. And I try not to think ahead to the actual arrival of the baby. Are you sure you can be home for it?"

"Positive," Emma said. "We already booked my flight. I'll be home three weeks before your due date, and I'll stay after for a bit. Patrick is hoping to get a break so he can come home for a week or so, he doesn't want to meet the baby over Facetime."

"Thank you," Zoe said. "I can't imagine not having you here."

JJ interrupted them to hand Zoe a bottle of water, and Emma took a step back to allow them to talk privately. As she looked around the room, she couldn't help but feel emotional. Two years ago, she had been completely alone in the world. Now, she was surrounded by family and friends who loved her. This Christmas was different in so many ways, and she felt so lucky.

Her childhood holidays, with just her and her mom, had been so special. Her mother had made sure she got a present from Santa, and her stocking was full when she woke up on Christmas morning. Even if that had meant working extra, or going without herself, she had found a way to make the day special. They had spent the weeks before Christmas making decorations, baking cookies, and singing carols, creating memories that helped her get through the years when she had been alone.

Now she was making new memories, which were just as special to her. All of her hardships had led her to this life, this love, and she couldn't be more grateful. If she had known over those years that this was waiting for her, it would have made them easier to bear. But at least the pain and loss had softened, leaving a memory of a mother who loved her, and a future that looked bright.

***

They played games that Emma and Patrick had organized before they all sat down to a dinner provided by Kendra and Zoe through Palace Plates. The Monahans had headed home after dessert, Maggie thrilled to have a child at home again to help hang the stockings and put out cookies. Eve had rolled her eyes slightly when Santa had been brought up but had a smile on her face that suggested she was excited about what the next day would bring.

"Should we exchange some presents tonight?" Stella asked, looking at the giant pile under the tree. "I'm afraid if we wait until tomorrow, we won't get through them all."

"Yes, presents!" Calle jumped up and down, clapping her hands.

"Maybe we can do our Secret Santa exchange, and the kids can open one each?" Kendra suggested, giving Calle a hand signal to calm down.

"That works," Jake said, taking a seat with Izzie on his lap.

"Who wants to go first?" Ben asked, winking at Calle.

"Me! I do," she cried out, making all the adults laugh.

Emma watched as Patrick pulled a gift from under the tree and hid a smile, knowing what was inside. He handed it to his niece, who looked disappointed at the small size of the box. "This is for you," he said. "But really, everyone. I want you to open it."

Calle ripped into the paper with glee, almost missing the paper that was inside the box. Charlie, who was sitting next to her, grabbed it as it floated toward the floor. "Munchkin, you dropped this."

"Thanks, Charlie," she replied, beaming at him. Her brow furrowed as she read, then erupted into a grin. "Really, Uncle Patty? We're going to Disney World?"

"Yes," he said, nodding. "Emma and I planned the whole thing."

"Does this mean I'm going to Disney World," Dan asked in a stage whisper.

"You are," Patrick said with a nod. "Mom and Dad too. And Jake, Shea, if you want? We included you, but if it's too much for you, Jake, we understand."

"No, I think I can make it work, if Charlie wants to go," Jake said. "I feel bad that we've never gone."

"I'd like to, if we can," Charlie said. "You know I love a roller coaster."

"This is too much, Patrick," Kendra said, studying the paper.

"No, it's not," he said. "I'm happy to do it. Emma and I will join you for a few days, but I don't want to make it too crazy. I want you to be able to enjoy it."

"We'll enjoy it more if you're both there," Stella said.

Calle continued doling out gifts purchased by Patrick and Emma, including a weekend trip to Boston for Charlie to see the Bruins play, and a trip to a famous doll store in New York for Calle. He also presented Shea with his Secret Santa gift, which was a housekeeper who could also act as a nanny

198

if required. Even though Shea tried to protest, Emma could see the relief on her face at the gift.

"I'm not following Patrick and Emma's gifts," Dan said, sitting back in his chair. "Who wants to go next?"

"I can go," Jake said, standing and taking a small box from under the tree. He cleared his throat and looked down, his service dog at his side offering support. The usually confident, stoic Jake looked to be unsure of himself as he shuffled the present from hand to hand. "I got the hardest person. Shopping for Patrick is impossible, because there's nothing he doesn't already have or can't get for himself. But I realized there was one thing that he wanted, and maybe I could help with it."

He handed the package to Patrick, who stood and hugged his brother quickly. Jake took his seat again, Shea reaching for his hand as Patrick unwrapped. When he opened the box and pulled out a piece of paper, he turned to his brother with a question on his face. "What does this mean?"

"I got ordained online," Jake said. "Emma mentioned how much you wanted a private wedding, and how hard it would be. I know you both got distracted when Eve appeared, and you ran out of time to plan something. I thought if I could do it here, at your house, maybe it would be easier. You don't have to if it doesn't sound like something you would want. If you would rather have a big wedding, I understand. But I bribed the town clerk to come out here the day after Christmas to do your marriage certificate privately, so you won't have to go to town hall. Between that and my being able to do the ceremony, you could get married without the press finding out.

And on a selfish note, I'd really like to do this for you. I missed a lot over the years I was gone, and I know how much you all did to hold things down for me here. This is a small way to repay you and to be present for one of the biggest days of your life. And since I think I was the hardest on Emma when she first appeared in your life, I wanted to be the one to officially make her a part of our family."

Patrick looked at his brother, and then down at the paper again, before turning to Emma. She was battling her own emotions at the gesture, knowing that witnessing this moment between the brothers would remain in her memory forever. The entire room had fallen silent, watching Patrick and waiting for him to speak.

"What do you say, my love? Want to get married next week?" Patrick grinned at her as he asked, the glimmer of tears in his eyes due to his brother's emotional speech. Emma was finding it difficult to speak herself, so she just nodded, then squealed as he pulled her up and into his arms.

The entire room erupted at once, with everyone talking at the same time. In the middle of the chaos, Patrick hugged Jake again, the brothers exchanging quiet words as they did. Once they let go, Emma pulled Jake in for her own hug. "Thank you," she whispered in his ear. "You have no idea how much this means to me. To us."

"Right back at you," he said. "It means a lot to me to do this for him, and to set things right with you."

"You came to my rescue the night my father showed up and scared the daylights out of me," Emma reminded him. "I thought we were even after that."

"Even, maybe. But I hope this will make you see that I'm happy you're in Patrick's life," he said. "I've never seen him so content, and you're to thank for that."

Shea joined them, putting her arm around Jake's waist and leaning into him when he threw an arm over her shoulders. "Such a romantic," she said. "I love everything about this."

"You bring it out in me," he said, kissing her on the head. He met Emma's eyes again before he spoke. "I can see the differences in my life since I met Shea, and they are all positive. You do the same for Patrick."

"Positive differences for both of us," Shea said. "And I agree, you two are perfect together. Are you really going to be able to pull this off before you have to leave for Scotland?"

"I hope so," Emma said. "I can't think of a better way to cap off the Christmas season. There can't be that much to it, right?"

Chapter 19

Patrick closed the door behind his father, after having helped his family load their cars up with some of their gifts. Since they would all return the next day, there were still piles of presents to be opened, but they hadn't needed to rush through it all. Calle had been anxious to get home and put out cookies for Santa, and the adults were hoping to get some sleep before the youngest woke them up early on Christmas Day.

"Did you have a nice night?" Patrick asked as he came back into the room, pulling Emma down onto the couch with him.

"I did," she said. "I still can't believe Jake thought of doing that. It's so sweet, and I'm really excited."

"I am too," he said. "But I realized I put you on the spot. Would you rather do something else?"

"No," she said, shaking her head. "As long as Zoe is there, and your family, that's all I need. Even thinking about planning a wedding while you were on location was stressful, never mind trying to keep it quiet. This is so much better."

"I only have one worry," he said.

"What?"

"I want you to have the dress of your dreams, and this probably won't give you time," he said.

"Maria already took care of it," she said, smiling at him. "When she came here, she brought wedding dresses."

"Are you serious?"

"Yes," she said. "I don't know if she's psychic or just brilliant, but she said it was the best opportunity for me to try on dresses without anyone knowing. She stayed and altered it with her assistants, so it's already upstairs."

"How have I not seen it?"

"I put it in the closet in a spare room," she said. "I didn't think you would go looking in there. I don't want you to see it until the day of."

"That makes sense," he said. "I'm relieved. Maria comes to the rescue again."

"She always does," Emma said. She yawned and rubbed at her eyes. "I'm exhausted. Should we do our stockings and go to bed?"

"I have one gift that I was thinking of giving you tonight," he said. "But if you're too tired, it can wait until the morning."

"No, I can stay up," she said, sitting up straighter. "If you want to do it now, I mean."

He grabbed it from under the tree and handed it to her, the box was short and thin and neatly wrapped. It felt light in his hand, and he watched as she weighed it on hers. "I wanted to do something special for you, because I know the last few years have been tough," he said. "And I know how much you miss your mom. This is my way of bringing her to you for Christmas."

Emma's hands shook as she pulled off the paper and found a USB drive inside the box. She held it up in the air with a questioning look on her face. Without a word, he took it from her and plugged it into the TV, then used the remote to start the video playing once he was sitting next to her again. Emma gasped when a picture of her as a baby, her mom holding her, came on the screen. A second later, a woman's voice came through the speakers.

"Hello, my darling daughter. I hope you're having a good day. I just called to say that I love you. I'll see you later."

Emma choked out a sob at hearing her mother's voice, and the video continued with more pictures of her and her mother, voicemail messages playing over each one. A short video clip played, showing Emma as a toddler with her mother, dancing at a barbecue. Another picture showed Emma learning to ride a bike, her mom holding the seat. A video from Emma's thirteenth birthday, with her mom presenting her with a cake while she sang. She could remember the moment, worried that her friends would think she was a loser for the homemade cake. Now she wished she could go back into that moment and savor it. The final picture was of her and her mother with their arms around each other in front of a Christmas tree, shortly before her death.

"Hi honey, I hope you're having a good day. It looks like nice weather this afternoon, so I was thinking you could meet me, and we could go get our Christmas tree today? I know it's a little early, but it's the best time of year. Since Zoe is coming to visit this weekend, we can decorate it all together and get the season off on a good note. I'll see you soon. I love you."

As the screen went black, Emma pitched herself at him. He held her tight, waiting until her tears slowed before speaking. "Was it too much? I'm sorry if that was too painful."

"Too painful?" she asked. "It was perfect. I feel like she was just here with me. You have no idea how much it means to me that you did this. I don't even know how you did."

"Zoe helped with some pictures," he said. "And you had all those old recordings of voicemails and videos you were afraid you would lose. We have this thumb drive, and there is a second one in my safe deposit box. It's also in the cloud, which the guy who created it assured me is very safe. So you'll always have a piece of your mom with you."

"This is the best gift I've ever gotten," she said. "I can't get over how thoughtful you are, and how lucky I am."

"I'm the lucky one," he said. "I love you so much."

"I love you too," she said. "Can we watch it again before bed?"

***

It had been well after midnight by the time they finished watching the video for the fourth time and then filled each other's stockings. Patrick had taken Emma's into his office, where he had everything stashed in his closet. Finding a way to hang them without the other person seeing had left them in fits of laughter, lightening the mood after the tears during the video. They had finally decided to walk toward the stairs with their eyes tightly shut to avoid seeing their stocking before morning. The thought of it brought a smile to Patrick's face as he slowly woke up, catching sight of snow falling outside the window. Emma was still sound asleep next to him, so he stayed still rather than getting up and waking her.

He replayed the night before, when Jake had given him his gift. It was the last thing he had expected, but exactly what he needed. His brother had removed the stress from the wedding planning and made it so he could go into his movie shoot with the most important thing in his life taken care of. He hadn't wanted to admit it to anyone, but not knowing when the wedding would take place, and knowing what a spectacle it would be, had been causing him sleepless nights. Knowing that it would happen here, and they would be married when they left town, filled him with a sense of happiness and relief.

Emma rolled toward him and snuggled close without opening her eyes but smiled slightly as she did. "Merry Christmas," she whispered.

"Merry Christmas to you," he said. "I was just thinking that this is your last Christmas without being Mrs. Burrows."

"I like the sound of that," she said. "Even if it will make women around the world hate me."

"They have no idea what a nightmare I am to live with," he said, laughing. "No one would trade places with you."

She lifted her head and met his eyes, then laughed. "Sure, keep telling yourself that."

"Should we go down so we have time to open our stockings and gifts before everyone comes?"

"In a little while," she said. "I had other ideas for how to start the morning."

                                    ***

It was snowing heavier by the time they went downstairs.
Patrick got coffee brewing while Emma turned the oven on to
warm up the cinnamon bread Stella had brought them the
night before. Once they had both, they settled in front of the
tree and looked at each other.

"Should we do stockings first?" Patrick suggested,
standing again to get them. He handed her an overflowing
stocking, then grabbed his own before sitting next to her. She
had filled his with thoughtful things that would come in
handy on their flight the following week, including new
headphones, a sleep mask, a book he had been wanting to
read, a card game they could play, and a portable charger. At
the bottom, he found new cuff links, with tiny horse heads on
them, which he loved.

She gasped when she pulled a small box out of her
stocking, opening it to see the diamond earrings he had
placed at the bottom so she would get to them last. "Oh,
Patrick," she said. "This is too much."

"No, it's not," he said. "They'll hopefully be perfect for
the wedding, but even if they aren't, they'll look beautiful on
you."

"You spoil me," she said. "I should have put more in
yours."

"Are you kidding? I love what you got me," he said. "It's
all stuff that I need that I would have forgotten about."

She laughed and leaned over to kiss him. "Sure, we'll go
with that."

They moved on to open presents, everything from new clothes to video games Patrick would play on set with his friends. They laughed when they found they had each gotten the other a new pair of boots, and Emma found the matching diamond bracelet waiting for her under the tree. When it came down to the last gift, she grabbed it and held it close to her chest, glancing over at him.

"I'm afraid this will seem silly in comparison to what you did for me with the video," she said. "That was so incredibly touching, and I know nothing could ever measure up to it. I wanted to get you something that would show a tiny little bit of the good you're doing in this world, because you so often diminish it. But I love you for those things, your generous heart and your ability to bring light into dark places. And I wanted you to see that."

"I don't even need anything. I just needed to hear you say that," he said. "Thank you, that was very nice."

"And all very true," she said. "Here."

He took the package from her and opened it to find a large book with a picture on the cover of himself, Emma and their horse Whiskey. The horse had been one of the first rescues they brought to the stable, and Whiskey had fallen in love with Emma at the same time Patrick did. When the rest of the rescues moved on to other farms, Whiskey had stayed with them.

He started flipping through the pages, finding horses and other animals they had rescued with their happily ever after stories. Intermingled throughout the animal stories were quotes from individuals who he had helped over the years.

The librarian, talking about how he had put a new roof on the building. Kendra, praising him for anonymously helping her purchase the Windsor Peak Palace when she was a struggling single mom. The youth center, acknowledging the families he had sponsored for holidays over the years. Charlotte Bryant, the mayor, acknowledging the public garden he had built years ago and dedicated to his mother. His high school principal, talking about scholarships he had provided and how they had helped students go to college. His eyes were welling up, making it difficult to read through everything, but he did the best he could.

"Emma," he said, when he had reached the last page. "This is the best gift I've ever received. Thank you."

"I want you to see how amazing you are," she said. "Not for what you do on the screen, but for what you do for this little town."

Patrick fought a losing battle against his emotions, wiping a hand across his eyes finally when he failed. "For so many years, people have seen me as what I do," he said. "You see me for what I am, and I can be fully myself around you. I feel like I have been holding my breath for years, and now I can finally breathe. You're my air, Emma."

"And you do the same for me," she said, climbing onto his lap and hugging him. "I learned what they meant when they said soul mates when I met you. You're what my heart and soul were searching for all this time."

"We probably should have saved some of this for our vows," Patrick said, choking out a laugh. "We'll have nothing left."

"I think we'll be able to put something together," Emma said. "And besides, this is better. Just between us."

He kissed her softly and enjoyed several minutes holding her under the tree before looking at his watch. "We should probably get cleaned up and shower before my family descends on us."

"I wonder what time they were awake," Emma said as she stood and started gathering up the discarded wrapping paper.

"Calle was probably up before the sun," Patrick predicted. "My guess is that Jake had to wake Charlie up. Teenage boys probably don't get up early for Santa."

"I don't know," Emma said. "He's still young at heart. And are you ever really too old for the magic of Christmas?"

"I'm not," he said, grabbing her again. "Especially when it's with you."

Chapter 20

The coffee shop was fuller than Emma expected when she arrived, although she should have realized that a large number of tourists would arrive to ski over the holiday week. She and Patrick hadn't left the house the day after Christmas, so exhausted from hosting two days in a row and the fun they had had with their families. Christmas Day had been a whirlwind of presents, food, drinks, games, singing and dancing, and her feet had throbbed that night. Spending an entire day lounging on the couches and watching movies while eating the leftover cookies had been heavenly after all the craziness of the holiday.

Eve had texted her late the night before, wanting to talk about her meeting with her aunt. Emma had asked her to meet for cocoa this morning, thinking it would be better to do it in person. She was just checking the time when she saw the girl rushing through the door, grinning when she caught sight of Emma in the corner.

"Hi," she said, pulling off her coat and scarf before giving Emma a brief hug. "Thank you for coming to talk to me."

"Anytime," Emma said. "Although you do know that Patrick and I are leaving next week, right? So, we'll have to do it over the phone for a while, but I'll always be here for you. How did it go?"

"It went pretty good," Eve said. "We're definitely not ready to be living together. Tori isn't sure she's even capable of taking care of a kid, so knowing I could stay with Maggie and Tim was a relief. But she was really nice. And she told me a lot about my mom, which was cool."

"What kind of things?"

"I guess she was always a little boy crazy. Tori told me to be careful if I am the same way, but I told her boys are gross," Eve said, shuddering in her seat. "My mom, I guess her name is Veronica, she was always doing things to make her boyfriends happy. Tori said they stopped talking probably a year before I was born. Veronica took off with a guy, who's probably my dad, and Tori never heard from her again. Tori tried to warn her that the guy was bad news, and that was the end of their relationship."

"Do you have grandparents, or any other family that Tori knows about?"

"No," Eve said, shaking her head. "At least, she doesn't think so. She doesn't really know much about my dad, so I guess there could be on that side? But she said her parents both died a couple of years ago. Which stinks, I would have liked to have met them. The thing that made me really happy was knowing that none of them knew about me. For so long, I wondered why no one wanted me. But Tori said her mom, my grandma, would have loved me. And that they would have taken me in. Even Tori said she would right now if I wasn't happy where I was. And she said she would have taken me as a baby if her parents couldn't have. That made me feel good."

"I'm glad," Emma said, smiling at her. "And you're happy with Maggie and Tim?"

"They are awesome," Eve said. She sipped the hot cocoa that Emma had purchased when she arrived, then licked a bit of chocolate off her lip before continuing. "This was the best Christmas I've ever had. I actually got presents, and a stocking. I've never had that before."

"They are really nice people," Emma said. "I've gotten to know their kids pretty well. Other than Colin, who keeps to himself. But JJ, Finely and Desmond are a lot of fun. And of course, you have my sister as part of the family."

"Zoe is great," Eve said, nodding. "And the others are too. Even Colin. He seems grumpy, but he also has a vibe that he would go after anyone who messed with me. So that's cool."

Emma laughed. "Always a good thing. And having JJ around doesn't hurt either."

"No," Eve said. "I can't ever get in trouble, because he would be so embarrassed. But also, kids won't mess with me."

"Are you worried about that? Starting school here in January?"

"Not really," Eve said with a shrug. "I've started new schools a lot. And Maggie and Tim have introduced me to some kids my age already, and they all seem nice. I even hung out with a couple of them for a little while at the gingerbread house contest. And they invited me to go skiing with them, but I'm a little nervous about that."

"We can get you set up with lessons," Emma said. "That way you'll be safe."

"I'd like that," Eve said. "Thanks. You and Patrick really went out of your way for me. And you did it even after I tried to take advantage of you. I'm really sorry for what I did."

"It's okay," Emma said. "If it wasn't you, it would have been someone else. Just promise me that if you need anything, you'll go to us, or anyone you trust, before you do something like that again."

"I will," Eve said. "And I'll never talk about you and Patrick to anyone I don't trust."

"Did you mention us to Tori?"

"No," Eve said, shaking her head. "She said she heard there were movie stars who lived here, and she's hoping that she'll get to meet one when she starts working at the bakery. She really liked Piper, and she's excited about working with her."

"I'm glad," Emma said. "I hope she likes it here."

"She wasn't sure about the weather, but said it was a really nice place otherwise," Eve said. "And that she was shocked the bakery made enough to offer her a house to stay in. I didn't say anything, but I feel like maybe it was Patrick who did that?"

Emma winked at her. "You never know what kind of magic Windsor Peak holds. Especially at the holidays."

"Thank you again," Eve said. "You are the only other person I know who understands what this means to me. Finding my family, even more than I expected, and having a safe place to live, is the greatest gift I've ever gotten."

"Well, since you just told me you had never gotten one before, it wasn't that hard," Emma said, teasing the girl. When she laughed, Eve laughed with her. "I'm only kidding. We're happy to help."

***

When Emma arrived home, she found Zoe, Stella, Kendra and Shea waiting for her in the kitchen. Based on the sounds coming from the lower level, she guessed that their significant others had joined in on Patrick's workout. "This is a nice surprise," she said as she hung up her coat. "I thought you would all be sick of me by now."

"Never," Stella said, hugging her tightly. "We're here to help with the wedding planning."

"Oh, good," Emma said with a laugh. "Because I don't know what we need to do. I thought it would just be here, Jake would do the ceremony, and we would all celebrate?"

"Well, of course," Zoe said. "But you need a bachelorette party, and a wedding shower. And flowers, music, dancing, all of it."

"I don't need a wedding shower," Emma said. "We have everything we could possibly need."

"You don't get to deny us the fun," Kendra said. "We thought of the fact that you don't need a single houseware item and decided we could combine the shower and the bachelorette. But instead of household items, we can buy you pampering gifts, or lingerie."

"You don't have to do that," Emma said, feeling herself blush.

"But we want to," Shea said gently. "You're always the first to offer to help with something, and you do so much for all of us, and the town. Let us spoil you for one day, please."

"Okay," Emma said. "As long as it's private. I can't have people finding out about that and the news getting out. We would be overwhelmed with reporters and paparazzi if it did."

"I talked to the florist who does our orders for the restaurant," Kendra said. "I asked for some extra greens and flowers. They are delivering to us tomorrow, and we had already told them we were keeping the holiday colors for another few weeks, so they didn't think it was odd that I would ask for more. We can put your bouquet together ourselves, if that's okay with you."

"Of course," Emma said. "And honestly, I don't need one."

"Every bride needs flowers," Stella said. "It will be simple but beautiful, just like you."

"Speaking of," Shea said. "I'm so glad you got your dress already. We thought we were helping you for the future, but it turns out to be a little miracle that you have it hanging upstairs."

Emma nodded. "Thank goodness for Maria. I would never have thought of it, and I would have been getting married in dirty jeans and boots if it weren't for her."

"We would never let that happen," Zoe said.

"Plus, you have a closet full of gorgeous dresses you could have chosen from," Kendra said. "Do you have shoes, or do we need to shop?"

"I can show you my options," Emma said. She glanced at the door to the lower level, where the men were working out. "They'll be busy for a while, right?"

"Absolutely," Kendra said. "Mike was grumbling about cookies and wine when they went down, so I think he plans to make Patrick and Liam work for a long time."

"Okay, why don't you all come upstairs," Emma said. "There's way too many to carry down here."

***

One whirlwind day later, Emma found herself wearing a tiara and a sash, surrounded by the women in her life. Kendra and Zoe had closed Palace Plates early, allowing them time to set up for a shower and bachelorette party that evening. Wine and champagne were flowing, with sparkling cider for the pregnant women, and there was enough food to feed a small army. Emma had opened the pile of gifts, finding everything from silky lingerie to a luxury spa weekend getaway to enjoy in Scotland, courtesy of Natalie, who promised that she and Holly would join her.

"This is all too much," Emma said, sitting back after unwrapping the final gift. "You all went above and beyond."

"We're so happy for you," Zoe said.

"And for us, since we're getting you officially as a sister," Kendra said, smiling at her.

"And we need the numbers, those Burrows boys are a lot to handle," Shea said.

"Are you feeling ready for the wedding?" Holly asked. "It's so weird to think that when we all go overseas, you'll be Mrs. Patrick Burrows."

"I probably should have figured out what to do about my passport," Emma said. "Should I be worried?"

"We're flying private," Natalie said. "And everything is booked under Emma Martin. I think it's okay to wait and officially change your name when we get back. Unless you won't take his name?"

Kendra, Shea and Stella all turned to Emma, looking shocked at the possibility of her not taking the same name they all proudly carried. Emma shook her head. "Of course, I am. I'd much rather have Patrick's name than my absent father's."

"Good," Stella said with a sigh of relief. "I'm glad to hear it. Now, what can we do to help you get ready? We planned the rehearsal dinner already, even though there's not much to rehearse."

"Any excuse for a party," Natalie said. "I'm so excited for a New Year's Eve wedding. It's so romantic."

"I kind of thought you would be engaged by now," Holly said, nudging her friend. "Mike seems like he wants to lock you down."

"Other way around," Natalie said. "Have you seen the man? And he's nice, on top of looking like that. I'm still amazed he gave me the time of day. I can't wait to marry him."

"Maybe you should propose," Stella suggested, making the other woman laugh. "What? It happens."

"Not when you're Natalie Cloud, and men around the world would kill to be in Mike's shoes," Emma said. "But I'd be surprised if Mike didn't do it soon anyway."

"We wouldn't want to rain on your parade," Natalie said. "Let's get you married off to America's favorite bachelor and then see what we can do about me and Mike."

"I can't help but notice my sister, hiding over there," Shea said, pointing to Holly. "I've never seen you so quiet before."

"It's only a matter of time before you all turn this energy on me," Holly said. "I'm just trying to avoid it a bit longer. I don't need that public scrutiny. Seeing what Nat and Emma go through is bad enough."

"At some point, you'll have to come out as a couple," Emma said.

"I know, but this works for now," Holly said. "It's not that we don't love each other or want to spend our lives together. But it's only been a year, and we both have our reasons to keep things quiet."

"You don't think the press will notice when you're in Scotland with him?" Natalie asked, with an eyebrow raised.

"With all of you around? And Patrick newly married? I could walk naked around the country, and no one would notice me," Holly said.

"Let's not try that," Stella said, laughing.

"I just hope they'll care less over there," Emma said. "And by the time we get home, the news will have died down."

"One thing I've learned the hard way," Natalie said. "Is to not let what people are saying run your life. You aren't what they say you are, no matter how many times they say it. You're the person you've always been. The person Patrick loves, who we all treasure as a friend. Don't let other people's jealousy cause you a minute of worry.

"You're right," Zoe said, nodding. "She's right. Just enjoy these days leading up to the wedding and then being a newlywed. Don't give it another thought."

Chapter 21

Patrick woke up early the morning after his bachelor party with a raging headache and a phone full of missed calls and texts. Everyone, from Sean to his publicist Missy, had been trying to get in touch with him, which was never a good sign. His brothers had thrown him a poker night to celebrate his upcoming wedding, and they had played well into the night. Between the late bedtime and the whiskey consumed, he was in no mood to deal with whatever had everyone freaking out. Fortunately, Emma had already left the bedroom, and must be oblivious to whatever it was to have left him sleeping.

After a quick, cold shower, he felt better about facing the messages. The first he read was from Sean, which told him in all caps to call him immediately. With a sigh, he hit the button on his screen to dial his assistant. Sean answered on the first ring. "Boss man, I've been up all night, and I was about to report you missing," he said. "You've never ignored me like this before."

"I had a late night," Patrick said. "What's up?"

"You're not going to like this."

"Lay it on me anyway."

"Someone got a picture of Emma and a bunch of women celebrating last night. It looks an awful lot like a bachelorette party, and everyone on your team is losing their minds. Your team, the studio, everyone. I've been getting calls all night," Sean said.

"Crap," Patrick said, running a hand over his face. "This is bad."

"You could say that. What do you need me to do?"

"Nothing right now," Patrick said. "Thanks for the heads up. I'll make some calls and do damage control."

"Call me back if you need me to do anything," Sean said. "I'll be on standby."

"Let me grab some coffee and then I'll make the calls. Can you send me the pictures?"

"Already did," Sean said. "Scroll back through all my panic texting."

Patrick hung up and then flipped through his texts as he walked to the kitchen. The pictures were taken through the window of Palace Plates, but even with the blur that came from the glass, it clearly depicted her in a sash that proclaimed her the Bachelorette. There was going to be no use trying to deny the fact that the party had happened, they just had to figure out how to stop it from becoming a firestorm. They were so close to having the private wedding he so desperately wanted, and he couldn't let this get in the way.

By his second cup of coffee, he had a plan in place with his team. Sean's original efforts to find a wedding venue could play in their favor and throw the press off the scent. He would follow up with the hotels, leaving the non-disclosure out of it, and let the news leak that they were looking at a spring wedding. Missy would also drop some tidbits that the bachelorette party had taken place early due to the movie shoot, and Emma having a pregnant sister. Missy had also promised to try to track down the source of the picture, although it could have been simply a tourist passing by at the wrong moment.

When his doorbell rang, he found his brothers on the doorstep, holding cups of coffee from town. "We brought sustenance," Jake announced, holding up the tray while Dan held a bag from the bakery.

"We came to help," Dan said. "We saw the news."

"I've been on the phone all morning," Patrick said, leading the way back to the kitchen. He gratefully accepted a fresh coffee and a croissant from the bag. "Word has spread like rapid fire. The studio thinks the paparazzi will be arriving any minute. They had finally left for Christmas, and now they'll be back."

"What does the studio want you to do?"

"Leave for Scotland," Patrick said. "Immediately."

"Why?" Jake looked shocked, and it was so similar to how Patrick had felt when the studio head had said it that he had to laugh.

"Because anything that will cause undue attention to the brand is a bad thing," Dan said. "Even if the old adage that all press is good press is still true. At the end of the day, this will bring more eyes to the movie when it comes out."

"That's what I tried to say," Patrick said. "They seem to think it will *disenchant young female viewers*', which is a direct quote."

"Which clearly is the target demographic for a superhero movie," Jake said, with an eye roll.

"Well, the ones who are there to drool over our little brother," Dan said. "But honestly, will any of them really not come if you're married? That seems a little far-fetched."

"I argued the same," Patrick said. "But there is no winning in those rooms. I told them I was getting married, no matter what. And when I arrive on set in a few days, it will be as a married man, so they should get used to the idea."

"Did they?" Jake asked.

"They seem to have come around. At least, they did once I told them they were more than capable of writing my character out if they really think this is bad for the series."

"They'll never do that," Dan said. "You're still the most popular character. And actor."

"That's why they changed their tune. Now they want to send a press team here," Patrick said with a sigh. "Have it all documented and then set up a media blitz for me."

"What did you say?" Jake asked.

"I told them the wedding is on New Year's Day," Patrick replied.

"But it's not? I thought it was on New Year's Eve?" Jake looked confused, but Dan laughed.

"They'll be too late," Dan told Jake. "He'll already be married."

"Should you move it up even more?" Jake asked.

"No," Patrick said, shaking his head. "I don't want this to impact what we have planned. We're excited about the date, and everything is all set. We're going to have a decoy wedding to throw off the rest of the press. Sean is working on that, making it seem like we'll be getting married in the spring. It might not work, but if it draws a few reporters and photographers away from here, I'll take it."

"What do you need us to do?" Dan asked.

"Act like all is normal," Patrick said. "If they think we're getting married in June in New York, that would be great. If you notice anyone eavesdropping, try to work that into your conversation."

"I can wear my Statue of Liberty shirt everywhere," Dan said. "Or better yet, I'll get Calle talking about New York. I can plan a quick getaway for us after your wedding, but the press won't realize that. They'll think she's excited about going to her uncles wedding. She's loud and lacks any filter, so she's the perfect person to spread misinformation."

"I just want to pull this off without it becoming a circus," Patrick said. "And now, I need to figure out what to tell Emma."

"You have to tell her the truth," Jake said. "Don't start your marriage off withholding information."

"He's right, as much as it pains me to say it," Dan said. "She needs to know what's going on. If the press descends on Windsor Peak, the more she knows, the better."

"We have two days," Patrick said. "That's it. I just need to make sure we don't have cameras outside when we're getting married."

"JJ can take care of that," Dan said. "And we can hire security for the bottom of the driveway. No one is going to make the trek up here on foot in the cold and snow."

"Could you take care of that for me?" Patrick asked, looking at Dan. "Or Jake, do you have any military buddies who can keep a secret who could do it?"

"Absolutely," Jake said. "I'll make a few calls. I'm sure they'll come through."

The back door opened, and Emma came in, bundled up in her winter gear. She grinned at the three of them as she pulled off her hat and gloves. "Is last night still going on, or is there another reason for the brother meeting?"

"We thought you both might need some coffee and carbs," Dan said smoothly, pointing to the items on the counter. "And we're about to get out of your way."

Emma watched with a confused look as Dan and Jake hurriedly pulled on their coats and departed, leaving them alone in the kitchen. "Was it something I said?" Emma asked with a laugh, leaning against the counter. She pulled a muffin out of the bag and pulled a piece off, popping it into her mouth.

"I really hate to ruin your good mood," he said.

"Oh, no." The smile faded from Emma's face, and she set the muffin down on the counter. "Tell me."

Patrick pulled her by the hand over to the couches, where they sat down next to each other. She turned to face him, worry in her eyes, and he hated that he had to ruin her good mood. "Some pictures got out from last night," he said. He deliberately didn't tell her what they were of, knowing she would blame herself, which was the last thing he wanted. "News is running wild that we're getting married."

"But everyone knew we were engaged already," she said, confusion on her face.

"I guess there is a big difference between engaged and married," he said. "And of course, everyone wants to be the one to get the scoop on the wedding."

"Is your team freaking out?"

"A little," he said, keeping some of it to himself. Remembering Jake's advice and changing tactics, he nodded. "A lot. The studio too. But we're going to see if we can manage it."

She sighed and stared at the Christmas tree, emotions running across her face. "What do we do? Should we delay the wedding?"

"No," he said quickly. "We're two days away. I think we can pull it off without any impact from the press. I want to be married, Em. I don't want this to ruin our day."

"Are you sure?" She swiped at a tear, then turned to face him. "I want this to be right for both of us. If you'd rather wait, and have it be a more public affair, we can do that."

"That's not at all what I want," Patrick said emphatically.

"Is that what the studio wants?" When he hesitated, she frowned. "Wait, they don't want us to get married at all?"

"They would prefer it to be more subtle, and not right when we're starting up on filming," he admitted. "But I feel like the fuss will be over by the time the movie comes out, so it will be fine. And they're going to send a team here so they can do a media blitz and pretend they are excited about it."

"I hate this," she said. "I was so happy thinking it was just going to be about us. Now it's about Hollywood."

"It's not," he insisted. "It's still about us. I'm not going to let them ruin this for us. In two days, we're getting married. I don't care what happens between now and then, we are having a wedding."

"What was the picture?"

"What's that?"

"You said there was a picture," she said. "You were here, downstairs. I can't imagine someone got a picture of you. And a poker night certainly wouldn't raise any flags, because you do it all the time. Which makes me think it was something I did."

"It wasn't your fault," he said.

"So, it was me. I'm such an idiot," she said, putting her head in her hands. "I should have just stayed in the house with the curtains closed."

"You're allowed to go out and celebrate with your friends," Patrick said. "This is someone else taking advantage of us."

"Who was it?"

"I don't know," he admitted. "But we're trying to find out."

"Do you think…" Her voice trailed off, and she stared into space for a minute before shaking her head. "It couldn't have been."

"Eve?"

She nodded. "Is that what you were thinking?"

"I did," he admitted. "But I dismissed it. You told me about the conversation that you had with her, and how happy she is. I don't think she would do this. She doesn't want to ruin the positive things in her life."

"I don't either," Emma said. "What about her aunt?"

He shook his head again. "Too convenient. We'll see what the team comes back with. I bet it's a random tourist who thought it was their lucky day when they saw you all."

"What do we do now?"

"Act normal, and get married in two days," he said.

"What about tomorrow night? You were planning to stay at Jake's for the night," she said. "Should we not do that?"

"We aren't changing anything," he said, pulling her close. "I know it's old-fashioned, and silly since we live together, but I want the first time I see you on our wedding day to be at the altar."

"I agree," she said. "And I was looking forward to having Zoe sleep over."

"We'll be fine," Patrick said. "What's the worst thing that could happen? Someone gets a picture of us on our wedding day?"

"I thought you said the studio was sending people to do exactly that?"

"They are," he said. "But I told them it was the next day. Our wedding day is just for us. If we decided to release a picture from that after, we can. Or we'll put our finery back on and let the media team do their thing."

"I'm worried about the impact on your career," she said.

"Don't be," he assured her. "I love acting, and I love what it's done for my life. But I could be just as happy here, rescuing animals and maybe starting a local theater to teach kids. I have more money than we could ever need, so I'm not concerned."

"You're sure?"

"Positive," he said. "Maybe this will be the excuse they need to kill my character off."

"You keep forgetting that he's immortal."

"Well, maybe he could find his own happily ever after and leave the superhero life behind," he said, kissing her on the head. "Because I know I've found mine."

Chapter 22

Emma had come close to canceling lunch with Stella a million times, but talked herself out of it ultimately. It was nice of Stella to want to spend some one-on-one time with her before the wedding, and it would have set a negative tone on the festivities if she had canceled. She drove to town, assuring herself the entire way that this had been blown out of proportion, and it would be a normal day in Windsor Peak.

Within thirty seconds of pulling onto Main Street, she realized how wrong she was. There were at least ten photographers prowling the streets, glancing in windows, and checking each car that drove by. She didn't know how they missed her, but she quickly turned down the alley to park behind the restaurant. Going in through the kitchen door might spare her their attention, even if it would likely only buy her a little time.

"Hey," Zoe called out when she came into the kitchen. "I wasn't sure if I would see you today."

Emma hugged her sister quickly. "Trust me, I almost didn't come. And now I see that I was right."

"What do you mean?"

"The streets are full of paparazzi."

"No way," Zoe said. She glanced toward the front of the restaurant as if she could see through the walls. "Want me to call JJ?"

"Not yet," Emma said with a sigh. "They're just looking right now. If they start to make a fuss, I'll need him."

"He always stops by for lunch, so I'll fill him in. I think it would be a good idea for him to walk you to your car," Zoe said. "Or Desmond can. He's big, and I had to ask him to come down and work since we're so busy. Luckily, he works from home and doesn't mind hopping behind the bar when lunch gets crazy."

"Oh, it makes me feel better that he's here," Emma said. "It's not like Stella and I could fight them off."

"I have knives," Zoe said with a grin, holding one up. "They won't get past me."

"I don't know if that makes me happy or terrified," Emma said, laughing. "But thanks for making me smile. I'll go see if Stella is here yet."

Her soon-to-be mother-in-law was at a small table in the corner, half hidden from the rest of the room and near a window that was blocked with Christmas decorations. Stella had sat facing the room so Emma could have her back to it, protecting her from prying eyes.

"Hi," she said, hugging Stella before sitting down. "Thanks for choosing this table."

"I saw what was happening outside, and I almost called you to tell you not to come," Stella said. "But I didn't want you to think I was avoiding lunch with you."

"I would never think that," Emma said. "But I did have the same thought. I was nervous about coming out after that picture hit the news, but had hoped the press wouldn't have arrived yet."

"In all honesty, we were both being silly. Our relationship is fine, even if one of us needs to cancel a lunch one day. We don't have to go through any of the mother-in-law drama, because I already love you," Stella said, reaching over to pat Emma's hand. "You're perfect for my boy, and I couldn't be happier for you both."

"Thank you," Emma said, choking up slightly. "I wish my mom could have met him."

"I know, honey," Stella said softly. "And I wish his mother had a chance to see him grow up and meet you. Life is cruel and unfair in so many ways. But I have to believe that your mom and Isobel are watching over all of us and sharing in our joy."

"I hope so."

"One of the reasons I wanted to talk to you was because of your mom," Stella said. "But if I'm overstepping, feel free to tell me to mind my own business."

"You would never," Emma assured her.

"You're very special to me, and I'm thrilled to be gaining you as a daughter," Stella said. "I know I could never replace your mom in your heart, but I hope that when you need a mother's advice, you know you can turn to me."

"I don't have to replace her. There's plenty of room for both of you," Emma said. "You welcomed me with open arms the first time we met and have always been so kind to me. I am so lucky to have you in my life."

"I'm the lucky one," Stella said. "Seeing my three boys find their other halves has been the ultimate blessing."

The waitress interrupted them to take their drink orders and rushed off again. The place was packed, and the waitress looked overwhelmed, to say the least. "I can't believe how crowded it is here," Emma said to Stella.

"We get a lot of tourists this week, and families looking to ski over the school break," Stella said. "I know the Inn is chock-full."

"Less room for reporters, so I'll take it."

"Speaking of, I had a question for you," Stella said. "I know the tradition of something old, something new, something borrowed and something blue might be out of date, but just in case. I wondered if you had something of your mother's that you could carry tomorrow night?"

"I do," Emma said. She touched the simple chain around her neck, which held thin silver hearts wound together. "I have this necklace that she wore all the time. She said the hearts reminded her of us, the two of us sticking together forever. It's very simple, and I wear it every day, but I plan to wear it with my wedding dress. It's my way of having her with me."

"Wonderful," Stella said, smiling. "I thought maybe I could offer something borrowed and something blue, if you don't mind."

"Of course not, thank you," Emma said.

Stella pulled two small boxes from her purse and passed them to Emma. "The bracelet is mine, for you to borrow.

Patrick got it for me when he first started making money. It's my favorite piece of jewelry, because I know he picked it out himself and was thinking of me, even from far away. The blue is from Isobel. It's the baby blanket that she had picked out for Patrick to come home in. She didn't know she was having another boy, but she guessed. She told me that she knew life wouldn't be so easy as to give her a daughter on the third try, so she might as well get used to a house full of boys. She found that blanket when we were shopping one day, and I made sure that Patrick came home from the hospital in it. I thought you might be able to use it to wrap your bouquet."

Emma touched the soft fabric and felt tears come on, making it difficult to see the blanket or the diamond tennis bracelet in front of her. Stella making sure that a piece of her mom and Patrick's birth mom would be with them as they got married was the nicest thing she could have done. "Thank you so much, Stella," she whispered. "This is so nice."

"Don't you cry, or I'll start," Stella said, dabbing at her eyes with her napkin.

The waitress returned with their sodas and took their lunch order, her eyes darting over toward the door. "I just wanted to warn you that a few of those photographers have been hovering by the door," she whispered to Emma. "We're trying to tell them that you're not here, and they haven't seen you yet. But some of the tourists are telling them that you're having lunch."

"Thank you," Emma said. "We'll be okay."

As the waitress walked away, a buzz seemed to go through the restaurant. Two photographers that Emma recognized from the red carpet had come in through the door and were eyeing the tables. Desmond had practically jumped over the bar to run interference, and his voice could be heard through the room asking them to leave.

The table of ladies next to Emma and Stella, who were part of Stella's book club and Emma recognized from around town, stood up suddenly. They were playing Mahjong on the table and seemed to be searching for a piece, effectively blocking Emma from the view of the photographers.

"We just want lunch," one of them insisted. Emma peeked between the women to see him point to an empty barstool. "I'll sit there."

"That's spoken for," Desmond said. The empty stool was located next to a man that Emma recognized as a local pediatrician, who was always friendly with Patrick when they saw him in town. Without a moment's hesitation, the doctor slid his jacket over to occupy the chair, stopping the photographer in his tracks.

"We're just looking for Emma Martin," the other said. "If she'll talk to us, we'll leave."

"Never heard of her," Desmond said loudly. "And if anyone by that name wanted to talk to you, you wouldn't be talking to me. Now I'll ask you again, please leave."

Two of the local teachers, who doubled as football coaches for the high school, moved toward the door, shuffling the photographers along with them. Within a few minutes, the teachers returned and smiled in Emma's direction, and everyone inside went back to normal. One of the ladies at the next table leaned over to Emma before she sat down. "We won't let them bother you, dear. You're one of us now."

Emma felt another wave of emotion, looking around at the residents of the town who had come to her rescue. From Desmond, winking at her from behind the bar, to the locals around the room who had helped her, she was so grateful. Any of their neighbors could have sent in tips to the magazines, or taken pictures to sell, but they had chosen friendship over gossip every day.

***

When Emma finished recounting the events to Patrick, he laughed. "I wish I had seen their faces when the football coaches were coming toward them," he said. "They aren't used to that."

"No, they aren't," Emma said. "And then Desmond walked me out to my car, along with JJ. There wasn't anyone out there, but it was a relief not to worry. I'm not leaving the house again until we're married."

"Good plan," Patrick said.

"Oh, and one more thing," Emma said. "I hope you don't mind."

"Mind what?"

"I picked up the tab for the people who helped," she said. "There's a rather large charge on the credit card."

"I would have done the same," Patrick said. "I'm glad you thought of it."

"To think that all we needed to thwart the press was a table full of mahjong players, a bartender, and a few football coaches," she said with a laugh.

"We might have to bring them out with us from now on," Patrick said.

"It might be a tight fit on that flight to Scotland," she said.

"Speaking of, I finished packing today," he said. "I left some stuff out that I will grab at the last second, but I'm mostly done."

"I wish I could say the same," she said. "But I'll take care of it tomorrow morning. I can't believe we leave in just a few days."

"You still want to come, right?" He looked concerned, as if she might have changed her mind.

"Of course I do," she said. "I'm not sending my brand-new husband off for months without me."

"Good," he said. "Because I would have flown back and forth to see you, and I don't know if I have that kind of energy. Especially with some of the action they have scheduled for me. It's going to be exhausting."

"We'll save the flights for when Zoe is close to her due date," Emma said. "Plus, Kendra and Shea. We have a lot of babies to look forward to meeting."

"And our own, one day in the near future, hopefully," he said.

"Let's hope."

"Not to change the subject entirely, but Sean tracked down the source of the picture," Patrick said. "It was a skier who had grabbed dinner next door and caught a glimpse of you through the window. She has a friend who works for TMZ, and it spiraled from there."

"I'm glad to put that to rest," Emma said. "I didn't want to think it was someone we knew."

"Me neither," Patrick said. "And I think we'll be left alone tomorrow. Jake has a few military friends who are going to come and do security. He said he trusted them with his life, and he knows they won't say a word."

"That's a relief," she said. "I feel like the whole town is rallying around us. You should have seen how they all worked to protect me today."

"They all love you," Patrick said. "I can see that anytime we go out."

"I love them and this town," she said with a smile. "This town has brought me all the good things in my life. When I look back and how I came here, I can't believe all that's happened since. Or that we'll be getting married tomorrow."

"Me neither," he said, smiling at her. "I already know it's going to be the best day of my life."

Chapter 23

"I had an idea," Patrick said, just as he, Jake and Dan were getting settled at the bar at the Palace. JJ, Mike and Liam were on their way to join them, a plan designed to distract from any rumors swirling about the wedding the next day. It would appear as though they were all going their separate ways when they left the bar, but would really all converge back at Patrick's house for the rehearsal dinner.

"When you start a sentence like that, it makes me nervous," Dan said.

"When you're nervous, you need a drink." Desmond, JJ's youngest brother, was behind the bar. He put napkins down in front of each man and indicated the empty seats around them. "Are we holding these for your crew?"

"Yes, please," Patrick said. Desmond nodded and put more napkins down, then started placing glasses upside down on them to indicate the seat was taken.

"What can I get you three?"

"Whiskey," Dan said. "Because I know my brother is about to make me do something stupid."

"Not stupid," Patrick said. "Inspired."

Jake snorted out a laugh. "I'll have what he's having," he said, pointing to Dan.

"Make it three," Patrick said. When Desmond went to pour them, he turned back to his brothers. "I'll switch to water after this. I can't afford to get bloated."

"Luckily, I don't have to wear tights anytime soon," Jake said. "Now, tell us your idea."

Patrick told them quickly, happy when they both nodded. It would be a lot of work, but he had realized the one extra step he hadn't taken to make the wedding perfect. Getting married in their living room by the Christmas tree would be special, but he wanted more than special for Emma. He wanted their wedding to be as special as she was. This would do the trick.

"We can help," Jake said. "And I can get Charlie, maybe some of his friends, if we think they can be trusted."

"I'm sure these guys will all help too," Dan said, nodding to their friends as they came in.

"I'm in," Desmond said from behind the bar. "I don't know what I'm offering, but I'm always down for a good plan."

"Appreciate it," Patrick said, smiling at him. "We'll text you the details later."

***

"Can I offer you any marital advice?" Ben had approached Patrick as he was refilling Emma's wine glass. His father was holding an empty wineglass, likely belonging to Stella, so Patrick poured more into that before answering.

"You're still basically a newlywed. I think if I needed advice I'd have to ask Tim," he said, nodding to JJ's parents

244

across the room. "They've been married for over thirty years."

"Hey, I was widowed," Ben said. "Not my fault. And Stella and I have been together longer than most married couples I know."

"That's true," Patrick said. "I hope we can be as happy as you have been all these years."

"I'm sure you will be," Ben said, patting him on the shoulder. "You're a good match. Stella and I are very happy for you, and for Emma."

JJ approached, and Ben excused himself. "Hey," JJ said. "Sorry to have interrupted. I just wanted to let you know something."

"Do I want to know?"

"Probably not, but I'm going to tell you anyway," JJ said. "Des just texted me, saying the reporters swarmed the bar shortly after we left. He said they're asking lots of questions and trying to get anyone to talk to them."

Patrick sighed. "I was hoping we would throw them off the scent," he said.

"Me too," JJ said. "I asked my deputy Jeff to park himself at the bottom of your driveway tonight. I know you're set for tomorrow, but I didn't want anyone to try to make their way here now."

"I appreciate that," Patrick said. "I can have someone run him down food."

"He's fine," JJ said. "And Desmond said that the locals are locked in, refusing to talk. No one will tell them where you live, or what's going on. Not that anyone else knows about tomorrow."

"I'm glad we were able to keep that quiet, at least," Patrick said. "I might need to think of another distraction tomorrow, if we want to keep this out of the papers."

"Des said he's been giving reporters fake addresses all night," JJ said, checking his phone. "He's accepting large bribes and then sending them on wild-goose chases."

Patrick laughed. "Good for him," he said. "Tell him I said thanks, and to make as much as he can off them."

"Oh, he will," JJ said, laughing. "Des can be very convincing, and he will get a kick out of making extra money off them."

"I need to deliver this wine to Emma," Patrick said, lifting the glass off the counter. "Keep me posted if anything else happens."

"Will do," JJ said.

Patrick handed the glass to Emma, who was deep in conversation with Zoe. When she thanked him and continued her conversation, he moved over to where Liam and Mike were sitting by the fire and joined them. "What's up?" Liam fist-bumped Patrick as he sat. "Still can't believe you're getting hitched tomorrow."

"You two are next," Patrick said. "Only a matter of time."

"I hope so," Mike said.

"Zane just texted," Liam said, reading from his phone. "He's on an early flight tomorrow, to beat an incoming storm. He wanted to know where he should go from the airport."

"That should help us stay below the radar," Mike said with a laugh. "Does he know how to be subtle?"

"I'll pick him up myself and keep him on lockdown tomorrow," Liam promised. "He'll drive me crazy, but it's worth it. If we call a car service to get him, word will spread. Zane said the press asked him where he was going, and he told them New York to see the ball drop."

"Speaking of," Patrick said. "Apparently, the paparazzi are running all over town. They all showed up at the Palace after we left, and Desmond is sending them on wild goose chases."

"Good for him," Liam said with a laugh. "I'd love to see that."

"I hope it works," Patrick said. "I really want to pull this off tomorrow without the intrusion. I'd like it if Emma could go to bed tonight and get ready tomorrow without worrying about what people are saying about her online. I won't be here to distract her, and the more the press thinks something is up, the worse they are."

"Can your team put out something to distract them?" Liam asked, looking thoughtful.

"Unfortunately not," Patrick said. "They think the best thing is to stay quiet. "We have a few fake leaks out, with Sean calling to scout wedding venues for the spring, but it doesn't feel like people are buying it. They might not even suspect that we're getting married right now, but they all want to cash in on pictures of us together."

"That's true," Mike said. "Nat said they are speculating that you'll get married in the spring in New York. She guessed they are all hoping to catch Emma wedding dress shopping."

"Anything that will sell," Liam said. "That would obviously go for more, but they are the hottest news right now. It will take a lot to knock them off that spot."

"Well, let's hope someone does something newsworthy while we stay quiet," Patrick said. "All I need is someone to steal the spotlight."

***

"I'll see you at the altar tomorrow," Patrick said, holding Emma close as they said goodbye. He would go to Jake's house for the night, and get ready there the next day, while she stayed at the house with Zoe.

"I'll miss you," Emma said. "Are you sure you want to do this?"

"Absolutely," he said. "It's going to bring us even more good luck. It will guarantee us a lifetime of happiness if we wait to see each other."

"Oh, really? I guess it's worth it, then," she said, leaning in to kiss him. "Whatever will make sure I get to be this happy forever."

"You know I'll do anything to make that happen."

"I do," she said, nodding. "And I feel the same. I love you so much. I can't wait to be your wife."

"I love you," he said. "And I feel the same."

"I guess I'll see you by the Christmas tree tomorrow," Emma said, tilting her head toward their living room. "Are you sure you don't want anything set up in here? I feel like we should have more seating for the ceremony."

"It will be quick," he said. "I don't want you to go to any trouble. Just focus on resting and getting ready."

"A whole day for hair and makeup," she said, smiling at him. "I guess I'll see what it feels like to be a movie star."

"I'd marry you with your morning hair and no makeup," he said. "But I want you to feel beautiful. Whatever that means is what you should do."

"I'll have no control," she replied. "Nat will be here, and she's in charge. We'll have a fun girl's day, although I feel like it will go by too slow."

"I'll see you tomorrow," he said. "Enjoy your last night as Emma Martin."

"And you enjoy your last night as the world's most eligible bachelor," she said, teasing him. "I hope the sounds of hearts breaking everywhere won't make it too hard to hear our vows."

He laughed and kissed her as a horn honked from the driveway. "That's my cue," he said. "But one more kiss. Our last one before we're officially husband and wife."

As he ran to Jake's car a few minutes later, a wide smile was on his face. Regardless of what the press tried, or people online said about them, he was marrying the love of his life in less than twenty-four hours. Nothing could ruin this for him. Jake glanced at him and rolled his eyes as Patrick climbed into the passenger seat.

"What?" Patrick asked, glancing around. "Why the eye roll?"

"You're sickeningly happy," Jake said, putting the car into gear. "It's a lot."

"Why? You are too, with Shea."

"I am, but I guess I wear it a little closer to the vest," Jake said. "You just exude excitement. You're like a puppy."

"Well, there are worse things you could call me," Patrick said cheerfully. "I'll take it. Where is Shea, by the way?"

"Dad dropped her at home," Jake said. "We figured you would need a little longer, and Charlie gets antsy when he has to babysit for too long."

"Two babies plus Calle," Patrick said. "I hope you're paying him triple."

"He used it as an excuse to have a girl over," Jake said. "I was a little nervous, but Shea reminded me they can't possibly get away with anything with Calle on watch. And she seems like a nice kid, so we have no complaints."

Jake stopped at the end of the long driveway where the Windsor Peak patrol car was parked. Jeff waved and climbed out of the car as Patrick rolled the window down. "Hey," Jeff said. "Congrats in advance. And don't worry; my lips are sealed."

"Thanks," Patrick said. "And thanks for keeping an eye out tonight."

"I only had to chase off a few," Jeff said. "I heard Desmond was sending people all around town, so that helped. But a couple found their way here."

"What did you tell them?"

"That the mayor lived here, and they must have the wrong information," Jeff said, grinning at them. "They all accused me of lying, but they moved on."

"Thanks again," Patrick said.

"JJ said you're all set for tomorrow?" Jeff asked as he turned back toward his patrol car.

"Yes," Jake answered. "I have some former military friends who are going to take care of things."

"Make sure they have my cell if they need it," Jeff said. "JJ will obviously be busy."

"Will do," Jake said.

"Thanks again," Patrick called out as Jeff opened the door to his car.

Jake waved and pulled away, heading toward his house. He drove a longer route home, avoiding any roads that would take them through town. Through the windshield, the town was still glowing with Christmas lights and gave off a sense of joy and optimism that Patrick soaked in. Tomorrow would be the best day ever for Emma, and he was excited to see it all come together. When he started running through the details with Jake, he realized it had all come together perfectly. All he had to do was keep her from noticing, and she would have an amazing surprise to kick off their wedding.

***

By the time he finished teasing his nephew about having a girl over and made his way to Jake and Shea's guest room, it was well after midnight, and he realized his phone had died somewhere along the ride. Scrounging in his bag for a charger, he left it plugged in while he brushed his teeth and changed into pajama pants. When he got back and slid into bed, he realized his screen was covered with notifications. Groaning, he debated ignoring it, but knowing he wouldn't be able to sleep, he grabbed it. Sean had been the most frequent and recent phone call, so he clicked on his number to call him back.

"Hey," he said when Sean answered. "This must be good if you're calling me this late. What did they say about us now?"

"That's the thing," Sean said. "You've been bumped off the headlines. What did you have to agree to do for him?"

"What do you mean? Do for who?"

"Liam."

"What? I was just with him. What did he do?"

"You haven't seen? Open Instagram, or any of the platforms," Sean said, laughter in his voice. "I still can't believe it."

"Did he get arrested?" Patrick swiped up and searched for the icon on his phone as he asked.

"No," Sean said. "Better."

When Patrick opened Instagram and the first photo hit his eyes, he couldn't believe it. Chronic bachelor Liam, who had sworn he would never put his relationship in the public eye, had been caught kissing Holly under a piece of mistletoe on Main Street. Patrick recognized the clothes they were wearing in the picture and knew that it was taken within the last few hours, since they left his house.

"I can't believe this," Patrick said. "I wonder if he did it on purpose?"

"You think so? I thought maybe he overindulged and thought he was away from the press?"

"I don't know," Patrick said. "He was fine at my house. And as far as I knew, they were going straight home."

"Well, they did after the kiss," Sean said. "According to the reports, it is already out that Liam has been living in Windsor Peak with his girlfriend for over a year now. The papers are going wild."

"I'll have to text him," Patrick said, switching over while keeping Sean on speaker. "Figure out what's happening."

When he opened his text thread with Liam, he laughed again. A screenshot of the picture had been sent, along with one line of text. "He did it on purpose," Patrick told Sean. "It was his wedding present to me. Said he realized it was the one thing I needed that I couldn't get myself."

"Well, that did it," Sean said. "I think you'll be able to enjoy your day tomorrow. Although Liam might have to sneak out of his place to attend."

"I'll let him figure that out tomorrow," Patrick said. "I'll have to find a way to thank him and Holly for this."

"Easy," Sean said. "Tell Mike to propose quickly. That will shift the spotlight off Liam and Holly."

Patrick laughed and said goodbye, promising to send his assistant pictures of the wedding, which he knew Sean would keep to himself. He scrolled on his phone for a few minutes, happy to see no mention of himself or Emma on any of the major sites. A Christmas miracle, even if it had arrived a few days after the holiday. As far as Patrick was concerned, it was right on time.

Chapter 24

Emma and Zoe had slept together in the guest room, at Zoe's insistence. She had reminded Emma that the following night would be her wedding night, and she didn't need to think about her sister when she went to bed with her new husband. Much like the sleepovers they had as young girls, they whispered late into the night. They talked about everything from the upcoming wedding to the upcoming birth of Zoe's baby, both excited about what the future held. When her eyes had finally drifted closed, she had dreamed of a baby with Patrick's eyes and her light hair, smiling at her from the future.

They slept later than usual the next morning and woke up to snow. When Zoe pulled the curtain back on her way to the bathroom, the whiteness outside made it difficult to see the trees. "Is this the weather you ordered?" Zoe called over to Emma, who rushed to join her.

"Oh, no," she said. "I hope everyone can still make it."

"We're Vermonters now," Zoe said, laughing as she made her way to the bathroom. "Nothing would keep them away. I wouldn't be surprised to see people arrive on snowshoes or snowmobiles."

"Imagine," Emma said. Visions of the Burrows family racing across the snowy mountain on snowmobiles had her giggling when Zoe came back into the room. Her sister stopped next to her, throwing an arm over her shoulders.

"It looks like the perfect day for a wedding," Zoe said.

"Said no one ever," Emma said, laughing. "But it's the day I'll marry Patrick, so it's perfect. Do you think everyone else will get here to get ready?"

"I do," Zoe said. "And I think the weather will stump any California photographers who might have tried to follow anyone. Mother Nature is on your side today."

"I didn't even think of that," Emma said. "You're right."

"Speaking of, did you see the pictures?"

"Pictures? Oh, no. I shouldn't look," Emma said, groaning. "I woke up in such a good mood."

"No, they aren't of you," Zoe said. "Look."

She took Zoe's phone and saw the picture of Liam and Holly kissing. The headline underneath declared that Hollywood's permanent bachelor was living a secret life in Vermont with an unknown woman. The comments were wild, speculating who it could be, with some people even questioning if it was Natalie. Holly's face was hidden by Liam, protecting her identity and making the reporters crazy.

"Do you think they did this on purpose?"

"We'll find out soon enough," Zoe said. "Holly is coming early to do her hair and makeup here, so we'll get the details. But it sure took you and Patrick out of the spotlight."

"If it was intentional, it was genius," Emma said. "And so nice of them."

"Let's go make coffee and see how long until the others will be here," Zoe said. "I'm looking forward to being pampered."

"And I'm looking forward to the breakfast my amazing sister will make me," Emma said, pulling on a robe. "Followed by the pampering."

***

The other women arrived in waves, delivered by husbands or boyfriends driving slowly through the snow. Emma fretted over each one as they arrived, taking wet coats and encouraging them to warm up by the fire. Holly and the hair and makeup artists were delivered by JJ, who ran into the house to kiss his wife before being chased out by the women.

"That was sweet," Stella said.

"He's even more obsessed with me now that I'm pregnant," Zoe confided. "But I'll admit the feeling is mutual. That man makes me crazy."

"Good crazy, fortunately," Kendra said.

"Holly," Emma called out to her friend as they waited for the artists to set up. "Is Liam alright?"

"Oh, yes," she said. "But he is still scared to drive in the snow. JJ drove him up to the airport bright and early this morning to get Zane and then offered to get anyone who needed a ride. He'll go back and pick up Liam and Zane later. It's much safer for all of us if the California boys aren't driving."

"That was nice of JJ. And I'm glad that Zane was able to make it, I know Patrick was worried," Emma said, smiling at her. "But I meant, are you alright about the pictures?"

"Oh, that," Holly said, blushing slightly. "He surprised me with that. But yes. He said it was the only wedding gift that he could give his best friend, who already has everything he could ever need."

"Really?" Emma's eyes filled with tears at the thoughtful gesture. "That's amazing. I hope you're okay with it."

Holly shrugged. "Okay with being linked to one of the hottest men alive? I think I can handle it. But so far, my name has been kept out of it."

"They'll figure it out," Natalie warned her. "They can be relentless. And once we arrive in Scotland, you're going to be exposed."

"It's okay," Holly said. "Liam and I were talking about how I might need to change what I do for nursing. There are a lot of opportunities out there that would give me more privacy, so I'll look into that when we get home. They also need medical people on set, so maybe I'll do that."

"You'd be bored," Natalie said with a laugh. "But it would be fun to have you there."

"We're ready," the hairstylist called out. "I'll take the bride first."

Emma moved into the kitchen chair, sitting patiently while the stylist slowly worked on her hair. It was pulled and pinned, curled and sprayed, for what felt like hours until the woman stood back and smiled. "Perfect," she said. "I'll do someone else now and make any adjustments we need once you have your dress on."

After an hour in the makeup chair, Emma was ready for her dress. The day had seemed endless, yet now she was close to the time they had agreed on to start the wedding. "Should we head upstairs and get dressed?" she asked the group, who all still wore robes with their hair and makeup flawless. "Patrick said not to come down until we have a signal, so we made sure we have everything we need upstairs."

"We'll go down first," Stella said. "I want to see you in your dress when you walk down the aisle. I'll make sure the boys know to get all of us. You and Zoe take your time, and we'll see you in a little bit."

The older woman gave her a hug as she started for the stairs, and everyone followed suit. When it was just her and Zoe left, Emma waved at the stairs. "Shall we?"

Emma led the way to the master suite, where her dress was hanging on the closet door. Zoe's was lying on the bed, ready for her sister to slip it on. "Should I get dressed first, or you?" Emma asked, glancing between the two dresses.

"Me," Zoe said. "It will only take a minute, and then we can focus on you."

Zoe disappeared into the bathroom and emerged minutes later in a silver gown that plunged at the neckline and hugged her slightly protruding belly. "I look pregnant," she said, standing in front of the floor-length mirror.

"You look amazing," Emma said. "You are pregnant, and you're glowing."

"Are you sure it's not too much? I have a black dress I can wear instead."

"Absolutely not," Emma said. "You're my matron of honor, and you should shine today."

"Okay, let's get you dressed. Are you ready?" Zoe asked.

"I think so," Emma said with a smile.

"I remember when I was getting ready, you and Nat offered me an escape plan," Zoe said. "I can't conjure up a helicopter, but if you aren't sure about this, I'll get you out of here."

"I've never been more sure of anything in my life," Emma said.

Zoe took the wedding dress down and held it open so Emma could step into it. Once she had pulled it up, she held the neckline while her sister zippered and buttoned her into it. Zoe stepped back after she was done and studied her, tears in her eyes.

"Oh, Emma," she said. "You're the most beautiful bride I've ever seen."

Emma turned to look at herself in the mirror. The dress was strapless and floor length, hugging her to the waist and then expanding into a full skirt. Along the neckline, flowers were embroidered in white and the palest pink string, continuing along the base of the skirt and down the train. The dress was both deceptively simple and beautiful in its finer detail, and she had loved it immediately.

Voices came from the hall as the other women were summoned downstairs for the ceremony, and a light knock on the door admitted the hair and makeup artist. They took turns making sure that Emma looked perfect, finishing just as a second knock came. Zoe opened it to find Ben Burrows on the other side, looking dapper in his tuxedo.

"Emma," he said, taking her hands in his. "You look beautiful. You take my breath away."

"Thank you," she said, kissing him on the cheek. "You look pretty good yourself."

"If you're ready, it's time," he said. "But if you need a few more minutes, the show will wait for you."

"I guess you're our signal," Emma said with a nervous laugh. "Thank you."

"I know we didn't talk about this," Ben said. "And if I'm overstepping, you can tell me so. But it would be an honor to walk you down the aisle. I don't have any girls of my own, but I love all three of you just like you were my own daughters. Shea and Kendra had their own fathers to escort them, and I hope that you'll allow me to do that for you. To step into my fatherly role a bit early."

Emma felt tears threaten at his words that she battled for the sake of her mascara. "Nothing would make me happier," she whispered. "Thank you."

"I'm going to go down first," Zoe said. "I'll see you down there."

Zoe disappeared, and Ben turned back to Emma. "You have Patrick's baby blanket as your something blue, your mother's necklace as your something old, and Stella's bracelet as something borrowed," he said. "This is from Patrick for your something new."

Emma accepted the box, finding earrings that would brush her shoulders. The diamonds were wound together to form an infinity symbol and shone in the light. They were stunning and perfectly complemented her look. Her hands were shaking, so the hairstylist took them from her and helped her put them on.

"There," Ben said when she was done. "Now you're ready to go."

Emma accepted his arm and took her flowers from the makeup artist, feeling the softness of the baby blanket wrapped around the stems. They started down the stairs, and Emma was shocked to find an empty living room when they got to the bottom. "Where is everyone?" She glanced around, expecting to find them in the kitchen or hiding behind the Christmas tree.

"This was Patrick's idea," Ben said. He led her through the kitchen to the back door. Outside, the snow had stopped falling, and a wide path had been shoveled between the house and the stable.

"Where are we going?"

"You'll see," Ben said. He took her arm again and helped her walk slowly across the icy ground until they reached the door. As they approached, the wide door was opened by JJ from inside.

Instead of the usual dirt floor in the stable, the ground was covered in white. Chairs lined the pathway in pairs, holding their friends and family. The horses were in their stalls, looking on in wonder at what was taking place. The stable was decorated in Christmas lights, with a gigantic

Christmas tree at the end of the aisle behind where Patrick stood. Lights and ornaments hung from the ceiling, along with boughs of holly and mistletoe. It was the perfect Christmas wonderland, and her dream man had done this for her. And was waiting for her at the end of a short walk, ready to marry her.

She walked the short distance on Ben's arm, kissing him softly on the cheek when he delivered her to Patrick. Jake, grinning, stood ready to perform the ceremony. Zoe stood on Emma's side, with Dan on Patrick's side as his co-best man, sharing the duty with Jake. And her Patrick, smiling through a shine of tears as he watched her walk down the aisle. He swiped away a tear before taking her hands in his, pulling her one step closer to him.

"You're the most beautiful woman I've ever seen," he said.

"I can't believe you did all of this," she whispered to him. "This is amazing."

"I wanted you to have the perfect Christmas wedding," he said. "And luckily, we have some amazing friends and family who were willing to help me today. Are you ready to get married?"

"Yes."

Jake cleared his throat, and they turned to face him, hands linked. "I'm honored to be the one to officiate today, uniting Patrick and Emma in marriage. As you all know, I lost my way for a while. I spent years away from my family, my son, and Windsor Peak, and I thought that was for the best. Through it all, I had a few constants. My family, and my brothers in particular, never let me get far out of sight. Dan and Patrick never gave up on me, and when I needed them, they came without question. They taught me what life should be about, which is family and love. Today we are celebrating those two things as these two start their lives together.

Patrick has the biggest heart of anyone I've ever met. He's giving and thoughtful, and I think we would all be surprised to learn of all he's done for this town. For so long, he was lost, and I can see that now. When I came back, and started to get myself together, I realized my little brother was struggling alone. Patrick was lost in plain sight, in front of the world. He was lonely and isolated by what the expectations were of him. He gave himself to everyone and asked for nothing in return. I saw him struggling to decide where he wanted to be in life, and what he wanted to be.

But when he met Emma, that changed. Emma came here with no ties to anything or anyone, and no agenda other than to find her long-lost sister. Now she's stuck with a whole family, and town, who adore her. Her sweet, giving nature perfectly complements Patrick, and encourages him to be exactly who he is. She allows him to be his true self in a way that he hasn't since he went to Hollywood. At the same time, Patrick represents security and family to someone who struggled to find that. They give each other exactly what the other person needs, and it's a beautiful thing to witness. They are truly each other's second half, and we are so lucky to share in their joy. Patrick, Emma, if you want to exchange your vows, we can get you officially married."

Emma wiped her tears away, and saw Patrick do the same. He waved a hand, indicating that she should go first, and she swallowed down her nerves when she saw the love coming from his eyes. "I, Emma Martin, promise to love you for the rest of my life. I will be by your side in sickness and in health, in good times and bad. I'll always be a safe place for you to be yourself, and I'll help keep you balanced the way you want. I hope to be the mother of your children, and eventually be on our porch watching our grandchildren play. I'll travel anywhere or stay here at home, as long as I get to be at your side. I promise to let you control the thermostat, and to learn the rules of hockey so that we can watch together. I will become a better person, for you and with you, because of the love you share with me."

Patrick smiled at her and squeezed her hand before he spoke. "I, Patrick Burrows, promise to love you back for the rest of time. I'll be your family, your best friend, and your biggest supporter. I promise to make you laugh and be a shoulder to cry on. I look forward to all of our days together, to building a family of babies and dogs and more horses. Through it all, I want to start the day looking in your eyes and end it holding you tight. I promise to always give you the window seat on a plane, and to always have enough ranch dressing in the house to get us through ten years. I know we'll change and grow together, and as we do, I'll be your constant. I love you."

***

Hours later, she was barefoot under her wedding dress, dancing in the kitchen to her favorite Christmas song with her new husband. Only the lights on the Christmas tree were still glowing, bouncing off the glass ornaments to create glimmers around the room. It was magic, and beyond her wildest dreams, that this was her life. That he was hers, and she his, for the rest of their lives.

"Today was the best day ever," she said, looking up into his eyes. "Thank you for making all of this happen."

"It was perfect," he said. "I am so happy."

"Me too," she said. She stood on her tiptoes to kiss him before putting her head on his shoulder. "Combining all the Christmas decorations and including Whiskey, not to mention the other rescues, was the best idea. I didn't think I could love this time of year any more than I did, but you made it happen."

"All I want is for you to be happy," he said. "I'm just lucky that I get to benefit and be equally as happy. I love you."

"And I love you," she said. "This was the best Christmas ever."

Acknowledgments

I love the holidays more than the average person. I turn on Hallmark movies and put up Christmas trees (yes, plural) the day after Halloween. I love baking Christmas cookies, wrapping presents and listening to Christmas carols. I'm someone who loves to give the perfect gift and see how happy it makes the recipient. I hope this book makes you, my amazing readers, feel the joy of the season! Giving you all this gift, to spend the holidays with the Burrows, has brought me so much happiness.

My parents, who always made sure that we had amazing Christmas mornings. From battling against all the other mothers to get me a Cabbage Patch Doll (the only thing I asked for that year–sorry, Mom!) to the year we believed our dad went to get donuts, and he came home with a puppy, every year was amazing. We did have an issue with the tree falling over, and have actually tied it to the wall some years, but it always made us laugh. I try to recreate the same memories for my boys, so they'll share in my love of the season!

Brendan, Conor, Timmy, Tessa and Emmy–you are the best nephews and nieces in the world. I love you all so much! You all make me so proud, with everything you do. Now that I'm done with this book, I can start Christmas shopping for you all! Jeff and Danielle, thank you for your unwavering love and support!

Cam and Calum, please stop growing up. The best thing I've ever done is becoming your mom, and I need you to know I am so proud of the people that you are. Keep being true to yourself and working hard to chase your dreams. And commuting to college is just fine, you don't need to leave me!

To all of you, my readers–thank you. Thank you for loving Windsor Peak and asking me for stories like this. For telling your friends and writing reviews. Showing up at events and being so excited about everything. It means the world to me, and it really does keep me going! I have many days when I think I should stop, but then I'll get a message from someone and it turns my day around!

And to my husband, who I recently celebrated twenty years of marriage to–it's hard to believe all that time has passed, and yet it feels like days. Your dedication to your family, the boys you coach, and to working hard to provide for us all is remarkable. Now it's time to start your Christmas shopping!

I wish you all a Merry Christmas, or a happy holiday season for those of you who have different traditions. I hope the New Year is kind to you and brings you happiness! If you have a chance to leave a review for this book, or any of the Windsor Peak books, I'd really appreciate it! Happy 2026!